I0658228

DEATH IN A LIVE FOREST

A BIG SKY P.I MYSTERY

DEATH IN A LIVE FOREST

John Holt

A BIG SKY P.I. MYSTERY

NEW PULP PRESS

Published by New Pulp Press, LLC, 926 Truman Avenue, Key West, Florida 33040, USA.

Death in a Live Forest copyright © 2016 by John Holt. Electronic compilation/ paperback edition copyright © 2016 by New Pulp Press LLC.

All rights reserved. No part of this book may be reproduced, scanned, or transmitted in any form or by any means, electronic or mechanical, including photocopying, recording, or any information storage and retrieval system, without permission in writing from the publisher. Please do not participate in or encourage piracy of copyrighted materials in violation of the author's rights. Purchase only authorized ebook editions.

This is a work of fiction. Names, characters, places, and incidents either are the product of the author's imagination or are used fictitiously, and any resemblance to actual persons, living or dead, businesses, companies, events, or locales is entirely coincidental. While the author has made every effort to provide accurate information at the time of publication, neither the publisher nor the author assumes any responsibility for errors, or for changes that occur after publication. Further, the publisher does not have any control over and does not assume any responsibility for author or third-party websites or their contents. How the ebook displays on a given reader is beyond the publisher's control.

For information contact:
Publisher@NewPulpPress.com

ISBN-13: 978-0692616888 (New Pulp Press)
ISBN-10: 0692616888

For my grandparents – Dora and Leo Reuland,
and Ruth and Lester Holt

What is it, then, which they have wrested from the forest, and which the forest yields to them so slowly?

- Antonin Artaud, *The Peyote Dance*

Against his will he dieth that hath not learned to die. Learn to die and thou shalt learn to live, for there shall none learn to live that hath not learned to die.

- *The Book of the Craft of Dying*

DEATH
IN A
LIVE
FOREST

-ONE-

THE LIGHT FROM THE FIRE in the small clearing flickers its wicked dance on the surrounding Ponderosa pines. Shadows move in and out of focus among the trees' long needles. The booming of an owl out hunting small rodents echoes off a nearby cliff. The sound of a creek bubbling and dancing across its rocky streambed mixes with the crackling noise of the flames. A pinecone bursts into light sending a stream of bright orange sparks spiraling into the sky. Billions of bright stars and galaxies shine in the eternal blackness. The yellow glow of the fire also illuminates the faces of several individuals standing on the fringes of the blaze. One of them holds a side-by-side twelve gauge shotgun that is pointed at two others positioned near a shallow trench that has the dimensions of a grave. The fourth member of the night's tableau is off to the side of the others, his facial features obscured by the distance from the flames. With swiftness associated with predators everywhere this one covers the distance to the two others being held at bay by the shotgun. He moves like a hungry mountain lion. Coiled within this swift movement is enormous anger and violence. A fist crashes into the nearest one's face. The man reels backward with the force of the blow as though shot with a gun. Blood spurts from his crushed nose.

The one with the shotgun is motionless. The eyes follow all of this, then the thinnest, slightest of grins creases the face. The one with predacious instincts turns to the remaining victim, who is now shaking and babbling words in a language only spoken by the damned and the terrified.

The predator and the one with the shotgun look at each other. They both smile easily – mean grins. This night's work is not yet completed.

~ ~ ~

The fish sails through the air. I pull back hard on the oars to give my friend more room to work the brown trout as it crashes and flies down this deep run next to a sheer wall of dusty-yellow rock. When the huge fish took my fly, Dirt and I had been discussing our friend Sam Jones being recently charged with the murder of another friend of ours, Mark Grace, but all of that sordid business disappeared like the line on Dirt's Peerless reel is doing right now. The Dog is up on the front seat, his large ears flying in the wind, barking instructions to Dirt as he plays the fish or rather as it plays him. The brown is well over two feet long, I saw that during its first leap. The crazed trout is well into the old reel's backing as it powers its way towards a wicked spate of cascades and mid-stream boulders. He tries to check the brown with no success. More line tears off the reel. I can tell by the pitch of The Dog's barking that things are getting desperate.

"I've got to pull out now, Dirt, or we'll get sucked into Red Head's Trap," I yell. Red Head's Trap, a quarter-mile of rough water, is named for a woman both of us know, someone who had chewed up both of us in the past.

Literally and figuratively.

"Hang on, damnit. I've almost got him," shouts Dirt as the trout reaches for the sky once again taking still more line from his ancient and banged-up Ari Hart reel. "See what I mean."

I don't, but this fish is closer to thirty inches, the biggest brown I've ever seen on the river, so I look ahead and plot a course through the roaring maze of whitewater that is now only a hundred yards away. I can hear the pounding and crashing of the river even above the wind. I can smell the damp richness of water. What the hell. If we die, we die. I can hear it all now over drinks at Dirt's restaurant:

"What happened to them?"

"Dirt hooked his fish of a lifetime above Red Head's Trap and that idiot Bouchee tried to row them through while Dirt hung on to the fish," and the speaker takes a long pull from his drink while those gathered around him lean forward expectantly. "Got pretty most of the way through, then Bouchee lost an oar and they crashed into a boulder. Smashed the boat to shit and they all drowned. Found the bodies tangled in a log jam down by Springdale," and the speaker drains his drink and asks for another. He's silent for awhile and then adds "I'll miss that dog. He was a good one."

My reverie is broken as we rode the crest of the first standing wave, this one about four feet high. The boat rocks and spins with the force of the twisting water, then we are in the air, briefly, before slamming into the side of a rock shaped like a bottle of Paisano wine. Probably Dago Red. The current holds serve. Both oars snap and are torn from my hands. Dirt is hanging on to the boat up front with one hand, his beautiful Hoagie Carmichael fly rod clutched in the other. The gem is worth thousands and belongs in a museum, but Dirt said "The guy built this to fish with and that's what I'm going to do with it." The Dog is not around. Nowhere to be scene. Next a huge whirlpool spinning out of control below the big rock twirls us around at about 45 rpm before shooting us into a series of smaller obstructions. We batter our way through this gauntlet, the cedar sides of the boat splintering and then we blast over and into a submerged rock that tears a three-foot hole in the bottom. The jolt knocks Dirt overboard, my last vision is of man and fly rod going head first into the river, feet high in the air. Then the boat capsizes and I am underwater. The sun is shining brightly. I clearly see the rock through the aquamarine current before I am slammed into it. Then I'm out.

The sun's heat and white light bring me around. The first thing I see is Dirt and The Dog standing in the river near shore. He's holding the brown trout at arms length. The Dog is sniffing the fish's gill plates. I also notice pieces of the drift boat floating languidly in the calmer water and Dirt's broken fly rod, in several mangled pieces, the reel smashed, lying on the cobblestone beach. The Dog looks fine, but blood is streaming down Dirt's legs.

"Hell of a fish, Bouchee," he said. "Between hauling your sorry ass out of the water and dragging this guy in, we had quite a time. Damn dog herded the fish to shore every time it tried to swim away. At least one of you is worth a damn."

"Right,

I slowly got to my feet. I ache and hurt all over. There is a fair-sized knot on my forehead, but other than that I'm fine. We've been lucky, especially when considering some of the other mayhem we've been involved in over the years. Only a gash on Dirt's leg and my bump, though we are out about seven grand on the custom-made drift boat. So what. We'd had dozen's of great floats in the thing and we still had Dirt's old beater fiberglass one. Just another day on the river.

I walk over and look at the brown. Thirty inches at least and maybe fifteen pounds. An old, scarred male with subdued colors - browns, blacks, reds, aged bronzes and whites. Dirt slowly pushes the fish back and forth in the water to revive it, but the fight has been too much for the trout and after twenty minutes or so he rolls over on his belly, gills working slower and slower in the water. Then they stop. The fish is dead.

"Shit," is all Dirt can say. Then he takes off his shirt. Wraps the big brown in it and starts walking towards the highway that led to town. The Dog rushes to the river and retrieves a small piece of the boat's wreckage. Then catches up with Dirt. I follow both of them.

"I'll have The Count mount it and hang it over the bar," said Dirt. He turns quiet as we push through the tall grass, grasshoppers flying everywhere by the tens of thousands. "I hate death. Too damn much of it ... My mother last winter. Grace murdered last week and now this brown. Only a fish I suppose, but it kind of brings things home ... I hate death."

Dirt had been close with his mother, Day. She was one of his best friends and when he received word that she'd had a heart attack while fighting a striped marlin in the South Pacific over by Fiji on her custom boat the *Up Above The World* (She actually knew Paul Bowles from her days as a rug exporter when she divided her time between Tangiers and Montana. Day considered that particular novel one of the best ever written by anyone), he took the news hard. Closed his restaurant for a week and got very drunk on Chilean wines, but one day there was a big ad in the local paper saying that drinks and food were on him the next night. So when I pushed through the door and caught Dirt's eye as he poured drinks behind the bar that evening, he looked up and smiled and I knew he was back among the living. The killing of Mark Grace had stunned everyone in our small town of 3,219 give or take a few. Everyone liked Mark. He never had much money, but along with his time and energy, what he had was there for the asking from anyone who needed a helping hand. Sure he drank too much at times and was always looking for ways to make a quick buck, but, then, a few of us had traveled those roads at one time or another. This is a place where most of us have at least a general idea of who most of the rest of us are and what we possibly are up to - not in an invasive or nosey way, but, like I said, in a general way. So, Grace's death affected all of Biederbeck's citizens to some extent. And the rumors that his dismembered body had been hacked up with a machete or even a chainsaw didn't make the situation any easier to take. Mark's murder made us all feel that Biederbeck and the world is now a lesser place.

"Well, this is a fine fish and it was one hell of a ride," he said. "We survived. Lived to fight another day and such bullshit." Just as we reach the road we see a rusted '63 GMC cattle truck coming our way. We flag down the noisy rig, climb into the cab and are back to town in minutes. The driver looks at us. He is up from his place in the West Texas Hill country where he bird hunts and lives alone most of the year, that is except for June through August when he heads north to spend some time on his small ranch at the base of the mountains south of town. He's about seventy, lean, tanned and tough. Todd Hollandsworth is his name. He looks at Dirt hugging that huge fish. He knows who we are and succinctly says "I don't want to hear about it," and returns to puffing on his Chesterfield and drinking from a can of Pabst.

Dirt walks off towards The Count's place, an old wooden shed that houses hundreds of broken appliances that are in deranged states of repair and disrepair - washers, dryers, refrigerators, gas stoves from before WWII, and so on. The Count loves to fish as much as any of us. He helped organize FWIK or Fishing With Kids several summers back. This is a small local group that he, Dirt and I are devoted to, one where we take fatherless children – boys and girls – from around town fishing along area rivers and even have a three-day campout at a nearby mountain lake called Zanzibar. This one is located above 10,000 feet and holds large, riotously-colored golden trout. We go up there in August when the trail is finally clear of snow to enjoy the company of everyone involved in our little program. In the winter we have fly tying classes for the kids. We want to pass on our devotion to the venerable sport and we believe that pursuits such as fly fishing may help these kids get through the tough, peer-pressured madness that is called being a teenager. Who knows? At least we try and the kids seem to love all of it. FWIK also helps keep The Count from missing his late wife, Kate, who died of brain cancer. She went through excruciating pain, but did so with dignity, style and always, when the pain would let her, a smile for everyone who came to see her. The two of them had a marriage that the rest of us could only marvel at. They were best friends, lovers, helpers, two of a kind, the best of Jokers in life's often cruelly-stacked deck. Her death rocked The Count, and all the rest of us. We pitched in and stayed with the guy until he got back on his feet – a little crazier than before Kate's passing, but all things considered, a grand person, and an honest, big-hearted, spirited soul. A source of laughter and optimism for the town. The Count is one of the best.

The Dog and I trudge home to our apartment on Biederbeck's Main Street. For the rest of the day my mind won't let go of the methods of death that Dirt and I talked about earlier. The one we barely missed, his mother's, the brown's, and Grace's grisly murder. Grace was someone we both knew, mainly from time spent in the bars around town. His dismembered body had been discovered in the Norton Mountains at a site he'd been logging. I drifted off into a sweaty, tormented sleep that is initially filled with horrible faces of people screaming for mercy while they were being hacked to death. Just another night alone.

~ ~ ~

All of this begins for me near the end of July when a woman bursts through the door of my office in the marginally stately Combination Block Building on Main - a ninety-year-old, two-story, brick structure with a large, fading cigar advertisement painted high up on one outside wall. "Every puff a pleasure," a smoke stuck in the mouth a well-dressed gent. The rent here is nothing. I have a bedroom, kitchen with a very old oak dining set that I purchased for cheap at Bob and Lu's 2nd Hand Leavings just down the street. The sitting room in the back has large windows looking out on the Norton, Buffalo and Weir mountain ranges. The previous resident bribed the building inspector and had a Yellowstone wood stove installed. The walls are lined with shelves that are filled with books, mostly first edition, first printings by writers that include London, Greene, Hemingway of course, Bukowski, Fante, Chandler and David Long. Books make me feel good about things. There's something about being surrounded by all of them, the smells of old pages, leather, cloth, the awareness of all of the brilliance contained within them, the wonderings about who read the books and what they experienced. I truly enjoy sitting in an old leather chair that my step-father gave me just before he died. Sitting in the rich red leather reading, perhaps *The Diamond Bogo* by Robert F. Jones, sipping some bourbon, smoking a decent cigar and occasionally looking over the top of the book at The Dog sprawled in front of the fire, four paws pointed to the directions of the compass. And there's a large room in front that I've converted into a modest office – mahogany desk that I feel like I stole from Bob and Lu's second-hand emporium two doors away, matching chair with cushion for my bony rear, a couch rescued from an old bordello up in Faro, Yukon that was being torn down, a pretty fast Dell laptop, small and old refrigerator that The Count gave me, Sony high definition TV (I'm right there with the cutting electronic edge), large, rectangular Moroccan rug in burgundy and tarnished gold (a gift from an artist slash rug merchant who recently left town to live with his mother somewhere in New England), an old chair with cane seat for clients, and more book shelves with more books.

I've lived here for a dozen years after fleeing Whitefish in the timbered northwest corner of the state. That place had gone belly up with the onslaught of tourism and rampant, big-money development. A free-form mountain town destroyed by greed and too many people moving in way too fast. Golf courses, boutiques, a ski area, lycra. Admittedly my Jim Beam inspired behavior, a couple of divorces and some hack-work articles I wrote on the trashing of the area by the rich and famous that appeared in national fly fishing magazines didn't help things any, but that's the way it goes sometimes. And there was a woman that I loved. The only woman that I'd ever loved. We'd split up. I was obsessed with writing, fishing and drinking. Too damn busy to spend the time, energy and heart she deserved. Losing her killed me a little bit each day and seeing her around town, knowing that we were through, hell, it was all too much for me. So I wandered over the Continental Divide and out onto the high plains here in Biederbeck. I was here in good and dusty and oh-so-delightfully windy central Montana now living easy, writing some – articles, novels, making a few bucks off my investigative business - divorce cases, insurance scams by broke claimees hoping to score some easy money or sometimes the other way around where the insurees had legitimate claims and were being stonewalled by the insurance companies, missing persons - and fly fishing with my friends. Biederbeck was to me the place that author James Crumley described in the **Mexican Tree Duck** when he said "I want to go home to a place I've never been." He got it right and that place is here for me. A high plains town with mountains flying all over the sky, some of the sweetest trout streams on the planet flowing through the land and a town full of open, reasonably decent people who don't care about a person's past screw-ups, aren't even interested, in fact. They've all got past weirdnesses of their own to live with. I can breath here and live in peace with myself, my past, present and future mistakes. This a good place to finish up the journey, to spend the rest of the years working, enjoying the good country and my even better friends. I'm grateful for what I have here, though I truly miss my Whitefish lady and wish that there were some way to get her back. But life rolls on and for the most part I'm happy, content and at peace with myself.

My loyal, non-judgmental companion of several years, The Dog, and I are watching Oprah on TV. The show is a fine one. Something about some guy who's written a book on the high incidence of unwanted pregnancies in captive dolphins and how this "interfaces (his word)" with teenage pregnancies in Cleveland. The Dog, a high-strung black-and-white Springer, will rest with his head on the end of the worn couch, jowls sagging, dark eyes half open staring at the mind-numbing images on the screen. He's called The Dog, because that's what he responds to, at least sometimes. I started out with Buford. No go. Moved to

Buck (*The Call of the Wild* influence here). Still nothing. Then finally this name when someone asked me his name and I flippantly said "The Dog." The screwball immediately leaped off the couch and into my lap giving me a look of adoration and long-tongue-sloppy affection. Who knew? It took me a while to realize that he really was watching TV. If I flick the thing off, he'll sit up and look at me until I turn his shows back on – items that include "Destination Unkown, Homicide Hunter Joe Kenda, C-grade slasher movies and way too many sporting events. He can always wait me out on anything of canine importance, never moving a muscle, barely breathing. Just staring with a look that says "Give it up man. I'm a dog and I know how to be patient." So, I give in and turn the tube back on. He loves baseball. The violent, frenetic pace of commercial-riddled NFL – punt, commercial, three plays, commercial, punt, commercial, penalty, official's time-out, commercial on into abject boredom, or the constant interruptions of the foul-plagued NBA makes him nervous to the point of pacing back and forth on the couch. But baseball he follows. I think he prefers the Cubs, because that's who I live and die with year after year. They are always on TV losing in ways beyond description or common sense. Great stuff but you have to be a touch nuts to slide along with it. I know about the languid pace and the long-haul, 162-game season-long rhythms of baseball. And The Dog and I both like fishing, bird hunting and wandering through good country. We get along well together.

When a woman appears suddenly that morning I am trying to light a Camel straight with a sputtering, sulfurous stick match, that also torches last month's cable TV bill, and a crumpled five dollar bill that I'd written the phone number of an acquaintance on. The corner of a parking ticket is burning some, too. I put out the fire with my hand, sending miniature smoke signals towards the nicotine-stained copper ceiling. I'm trying to put this addiction behind me, but like many others, I'm having a spot of trouble, but I'll stay with it until I get it right.

Despite the worry and fear, the red-rimmed eyes and the rumpled clothing, the woman is attractive. Tan, early-forties, tall, shoulder-length, light brown hair, lean but not skinny. Even with the obvious stress she seems to be experiencing, she moves with grace and dignity, with a sense of control and style. Her tired eyes glow with life, determination, strength. I've seen her around town a few times, like sitting at the bar in Ray's Bleachers sipping Glennfidditch and talking about painting with my friend Dick "Dirt" Tidrow, who owns the restaurant.

Tidrow got his nickname from a time before I landed in town. A time when a wealthy woman from back east capriciously backed out on a deal where Dirt was to paint a series of large landscapes for her for real money. Many thousands of dollars. I'd heard more than a quarter-million from several people in town. She informed him of her change of mind in a letter followed by an icy, terse phone call. No reason. She just didn't want the paintings anymore. Adding to the wreckage was the fact that Dirt was in love with her and planned to ask the woman to marry him the next time she came out West to visit. Dirt was obsessed like me, only with his painting. We were both blind all too often to the righteous needs of others and he and I along with our women friends paid a high price for these self-absorptions. Maybe someday both Dirt and I would learn how to do better. Maybe, just maybe. After the bad news that also conveyed a not-so-subtle implication in her tome that she was no longer interested in seeing Dirt ever again, he'd hung up the receiver, headed down to the river that cruises through town, filled up a garbage bag with sandy mud from the stream bank, drove back in his beater 1977 Oldsmobile Cutlass Supreme, hauled the paintings out of his studio on Main, lined them up against the masonry wall beneath the glow of an intense sun and flung the dirt at his art until the images were ruined. He then placed the remains in the middle of the street, piled back in the Olds, quart of whiskey in one hand, car keys in the other, and drove over them, back and forth, until they were nothing more than strips of grimy, shredded canvas. I understand this type of behavior. Years ago when a beautiful blonde named Amy left me for a rock guitarist (life can be so inexplicably cruel at times) I took the pages of a novel called *Chief Oskosh* (named after a dreadful beer made in Wisconsin years ago) that I was nearly finished with and flung them from the Higgins Street Bridge in Missoula and watched them swirl, sink and soggily float downriver while drinking from a pint of Old Grand Dad. The novel was a bad one and no great loss, but at the time my actions seemed heart-breakingly heroic, at least to me at the time. Pretty damn lame as I look back on the incident now. He then went back to his restaurant, closed the place for three days, drank wine and read Charles Bukowski, including *Play The Piano Drunk Like A Percussion Instrument Until The*

Fingers Bleed A Bit three times. At least this is what he claimed the one time I asked him about any of this. The sound of The Ford Brothers, Mozart and Amos Garrett humming through the walls was the only sign of life in the place. No lights. When he finally emerged Tidrow, now nicknamed Dirt by The Count, was a calmer, more patient soul. He'd changed and eventually came to lament the destruction of his work, along with the frustration and anger that led to the wasteful act. He has not completely gotten over his anger about the raw deal, but he has accepted that these things happen. Dirt doesn't paint much anymore, but when he does, the works are large, open and secretive, like the land around Biederbeck. And he runs a damn good restaurant. He named his place after a bar called Ray's Bleachers in Chicago located on a street corner behind right-centerfield at Wrigley Field where the Cubs do whatever it is they do. He strongly denies that he is or ever has been a Cubs' fan or even likes anything about baseball, but some of us know better. Those with a disease are well aware of the symptoms in others. Naming his place Ray's is a dead giveaway. Beside this business, he likes to chase trout when he thinks that no one is looking. A lot of us are that way. And Dirt is my friend. There are times when I work on the whiskey in his place with single and serious intent, aiming to get hammered and pass out on the bar. He always appears several drinks before touchdown and somehow coerces me back to my place, though the only thing I will normally remember is waking up fully-clothed on my bed covered with a blanket, the Dog asleep on a smaller version of the Moroccan carpet next to the bed. Dirt has done this big favor, and it is big in a small town where silly transgressions tend to destroy at least the illusion of privacy and autonomy in this life, a few more times than several.

"You're Ed Bouchee, the private detective?"

Before I can answer, she starts crying. I've never seen anyone actually burst into tears before, but she sure as hell does. They cascade from her eyes and roll down her flushed cheeks. She shudders as she tries unsuccessfully to control her emotions. At least she is making a try at it. I've learned to appreciate any effort in control over the years.

Handkerchiefs disgust me for obvious reasons and I am out of tissues, so I walk over to the old refrigerator that also serves as The Dog's deluxe TV stand. When I grab a clean towel hanging from the door handle, a couple of black-and-white photos of twenty-inch-plus brown trout I've fooled on the Hart River just north of town break loose from the aging tape, it has been awhile since I've fooled anything as large as these fish, actually, since I've fooled anything or anyone. They fall to the floor, sliding beneath the machine. I hand her the towel. She dries her eyes while I fish out the trout mug shots with a cleaning rod for my S&W .357 magnum. The Dog is asleep, snoring fairly sedately, front paws flicking in dreamland pursuit of some wild animal. Probably a ground squirrel or a marmot. He won't wake up until 3:35 when the Beverly Hillbillies come on. Every weekday he snaps to at this time and waits for me to turn on the tube. Amazing. Apparently Jethro amuses him. A frightening thought. I offer my potential client a chair and after a few more seconds of snuffles and whimpers, she sits down and looks at the mess on my desk. Crumpled cigarette packs, full ashtray, fly-tying vice

16

with a partially-finished bug in the jaws, thread, cree hackle cape, grey dubbing, head cement, large patch of elk hair, shot glass full of completed flies, an old scorecard from Wrigley Field, legal pad and cheap pen, half-full bottle of Schwepps Bitter Lemon, a flock of parking tickets, the laptop, pocket *American Heritage College Dictionary* and a ragged copy of a biography of Sir William Butler. I lead a full life.

"Tying elk hair caddis I see. That's one of Sam's favorite patterns. He's my husband. Why I'm here," and more tears appear. "I need help. The police think I'm crazy."

"They think everybody's crazy."

"They won't listen to me and I can't reach the police chief, what the hell's his name? Jim Qualls. Maybe he'll believe my story. I don't know who to turn to. I'm desperate and you're the only detective in town. Dirt said that you are an 'incompetent clown, but worth a shot.' And that you were honest and stubborn," and she looked up with hopeful eyes.

Hardly a ringing endorsement, but better than what Tidrow usually said about me. We're friends but never much for complimenting each other's somewhat obscure and esoteric abilities. He plays with some high-rollers – old money, actors, musicians. I mostly play by myself. Hey, work is work and the cable bill needs attention, along with the rent, new u-joints for the truck, the phone and power bills, plus the happy crowd at the local bank wants money for a loan they'd made me for something. Perhaps the laptop. Other than these minor issues, I was fiscally solvent. How I paid my way, this work, some writing, didn't exactly earn me fame and fortune, but as Buffett sang years ago 'I don't want the fame that brings misfortune,.' Not likely to be a problem anytime soon. I stopped working myself over about achieving any consistent level of social responsibility or productivity a bunch of semi-serious errors in judgment ago. I did the best I could, laid low and hoped I didn't hurt anyone in the process. In one way I got lucky inheriting enough money from an uncle who'd worked for a brewery in Ekalaka (a dying little cow town way out east of here) to buy some books from ICS that helped with the fringe aspects of being a marginally successful private investigator. How could I resist Sally Struther's lithium-soaked pitch on the TV commercial they ran over and over during breaks on the Travel Channel. Actually, Qualls helped me with getting the appropriate licenses and bonds, and gave advice to me whether I thought I needed it or not. With what remained of the money I started up Ed Bouchee Private Investigations or Eb-Pie as Dirt called it. Like I said, respect is largely a matter of perspective. With some rare luck, parsimonious spending habits and an ability to truly enjoy cheap cigars, even cheaper whiskey (Jim Beam is top shelf in my world) and a curious ability to take real pride in driving a 1983 Chevy pickup, I not only survive but flourish in a battered fashion. This despite the constant threatening phone calls from bill collectors. Divorces, snooping for insurance companies, somebody wanting something on somebody else, not exactly quantifying cold fusion or finding a cure for malignant disease, but the work left me plenty of time to chase trout and hunt grouse. I love wading the small high plains streams that drift out of the mountains and wandering through sage flats, weathered hills and wheat fields. These are times when the loneliness caused by old friends like self-doubt and a basic terror regarding what the hell I'm doing on the planet disappears on the wind. Casting flies like the elk hairs, hoppers or large woolly buggers to trout on a hot July afternoon or working brushy covers in the subdued, sherry-colored light of October kicking up sharptails with The Dog, sometimes just up ahead, sometimes way, way ahead, that is my notion of bliss, of heaven. Not much more is needed, only a slight excuse to run out and play in what remains of the good country around here.

The Dog groans and rolls over, falling on the floor with a sound like a sack of cement hitting asphalt. He looks around with obvious confusion for a moment before climbing back up on the couch with an expression that says "It could happen to anyone." He's snoring again in seconds.

"What's your name and what's your problem?" Admittedly one hell of a line.

"Liz Jones. I live up in Coltrane and I really need someone to help me. Even to just listen to me like they cared. God this is hell."

I know that Liz is Sam's wife. I've run into him fishing and at Dirt's place. We've talked about this and that over drinks a number of times, so I know a little about the guy, at least as much as whiskey lets you know anything about a person. A good guy. He's volunteered his time for FWIK on occasion, especially with our mountain lake campouts. He's a good man with pack horses and likes to do anything that's needed around camp.

I mention this and add that "I liked him right off the bat. As for listening and caring, I'm getting pretty good at that. We've got all afternoon and longer if necessary. Start wherever you want and we'll backtrack later. Would you like some coffee or a beer? Oh, and I want to thank you, belatedly of course, for that nice donation you made to the school library's book fund. It means a lot. We raised enough money to buy more than one-hundred books written by Montana authors. I think that it's important for the students to have a chance to read the work done by those who live here."

She nods her acknowledgement to all of this and a touch of a smile crosses her face. Biederbeck is small-town Montana. None of us are on the short list for sainthood, but most of us help each other out and do what we can to make town a good place to live. FWIK, the library fund, trash cleanups along the Interstate and state highways. A little bit here and some more there is all I'm talking about.

I pour a cup of the thick, well-cooked stuff and carefully hand it to her. Spilling the liquid on her could have HazMat overtones. She takes a sip and says "At least you make strong coffee."

Then she recounts a story that is, even by my arcane standards, twisted.

Her husband, Sam, is a logger. He is now in the state mental hospital at Turbid Springs. He is heavily sedated, closely guarded on a suicide watch and charged with murdering his timber-cutting partner Mark Grace. All of this I already knew or had surmised. Everyone in the county knows something about this one. I consider both

Sam and Mark friends in the way people who share a few drinks with someone on a semi-regular basis do. Small town. Big drinks. Everyone's a buddy and an enemy at times with everyone else. When, if ever, he will stand trial is up to the boys in charge of the institution. It is the psychiatrist's call as to when or if ever Sam will be competent to deal with the court system, all things considered these days, perhaps that will be never.

I've read about the case in the paper and watched pieces of the goings on during the local newscasts, but that was nearly a month ago. The whole thing appears to be ugly business. Grace is shot in the head with a deer slug from a twelve-gauge and then hacked up into several chunks - ah, the good life way out here in Montana. The partner's "partially decomposed body" (I've always loved the image this phrase conjures in my mind) was unearthed earlier this month by a couple of Qualls' deputies in a shallow grave dug in the rocky soil, and the site was covered over with pine needles. The coroner determined that Grace had been dead for maybe a couple of weeks, give or take. The weather had been hot during this time and the logging site faced south for maximum sun exposure. That's as close as they could come to a time of death. Nothing like detail to flesh out an investigation.

The O'Keefe County District Attorney, Fred "I never missed one in my heart" Lynn is locally well-known going on regionally famous for losing lead-pipe cinch cases. Last year a defendant was set free despite a signed confession and three eyewitnesses who saw him shoot his girlfriend at a local bowling alley in an argument over keeping score. Tough league. Lynn had somehow managed to violate the defendant's rights while securing the admission of guilt and a lengthy delay in bringing the case to court also came into play. Another murderer has been on death row at Deer Lodge for fifteen years and is currently on his fourth appeal. Lynn has publicly guaranteed the man's execution, so he'll probably go free soon. Considering these cases and others of a similar nature, I can well imagine that Lynn is in no hurry to have Sam Jones deemed straight enough to stand trial. The fewer times Lynn hits the courtroom the better is probably to be the DA's prevailing attitude.

Liz said that a little more than a month of working in an isolated sale up the Indian Creek drainage in the Norton Mountains had rearranged Sam's cerebral priorities to the extent that he no longer recognized her, or knew the name of his dead partner or even the names of his German shorthair hunting dogs. Totally over the edge. The cheese has slipped off his cracker. According to Liz the work had gone all right for the first few days. The sale was an easy one to cut, not too steep land along the creek about twenty miles up a dirt road off of Highway 17 that ran north-south just east of Biederbeck. Mostly Ponderosa that was simple to drop and load. Not a big sale, but with a little help from the weather coupled with the rising price of wood, there promised to be enough money in the work to pay some bills and squeeze through the winter. Sam is a gypo logger, one of the many private contractors around the state who scratches out a living felling trees on sites that the large companies aren't interested in. But with the cut-and-run, high-priced bidding tactics of the timber giants, sales like these are starting to grow scarce and loggers like Sam and Grace are becoming an endangered species. Sam and Liz always got by and there were rumors that one of them came into a fair amount of family money. When things were about to turn really ugly for the pair, just enough family help would arrive at the height of these desperate financial times. Hard to say what's really the source of the income. Rumors often pass for facts in town. They seemed to be pretty much broke, living paycheck to paycheck like most of the rest of us.

Sam and Grace camped at the site, saving driving time and gas money, a serious consideration at well over two bucks a gallon. After four days, Sam returned to the couple's home for some clean clothes, home cooking and related activities. He told Liz the work was going well. He did mention that he thought that there must be a grizzly in the area because each morning they saw fresh claw marks on trees near camp and large tracks leading to the densely-wooded slopes bordering Indian Creek.. The marks and tracks seemed to be that of a grizzly because of its size and the deep claw indentions ahead of the toe marks. Sam and Mark were both long-time hunters. They would know the difference between this animal and a smaller black bear. A grizzly in that area seemed odd to Liz because the Nortons are an isolated island mountain range and most of the state's remaining grizzlies are wandering around up north in Glacier Park and the Bob Marshall Wilderness or down in Yellowstone National Park. It is rare for the big bears to wander far out and across open country these days where they will likely be shot, hit by a truck or drugged and radio-collared by some maniac wildlife biologist with visions of grant money on the brain. Still, grizzlies do whatever they please, so anything is possible including

23

having one find its way to the Nortons.

Liz said that Sam carried a Mossberg Model 500 Mariner ten-gauge shotgun with a pistol grip loaded with 000 buckshot and rifled slugs stored in a rack in his pickup, so bears were of no particular concern. I ask how Sam has come by something of as distinguished and esoteric as this breed of gun. She added that he'd always wanted the model after firing one a friend of his had to drive off sharks around Cedar Key in Florida. His friend called the weapon "Big Bob," and Sam exclaimed that the flame from the muzzle went for five feet in the night. Liz gave him an identical model for Christmas a few years back. It would no doubt make one hell of a grouse gun, too. I also figure that the noise of the chainsaws and falling trees probably scared off the bear during the day. Liz adds that both Sam and Grace grew up in Montana, so dealing with wildlife is routine. They've been around big game like bears, elk, mountain lions, and mule deer all their lives. Still, a large grizzly can tear a man in half with a swipe of its paw, but then inner-city Detroit is no joy ride either. (My mother went to the University of Michigan in the late forties. She said that the inner city residents called every Thursday "Bump Day," a weekly time of frivolity when they'd knock all outsiders into the street in front of cabs, delivery trucks, buses, squad cars. Always something fun going down in the Motor City.)

So, after a night of good food, talk and intimacy, Sam drove back to the work, followed by Grace in the logging truck.

Grace had partied at The Nighthawk, a local bar of marginal repute that is a hangout for all of the writers in

John Holt

town who think they are some amalgamation of Hemingway and Edward R. Murrow. They've given themselves nicknames like Captain C and Tommy the Turk. Harmless but it is a bit old. The owner, Todd Hundley, is a good guy and builds a serious drink. I've been known to kill a few afternoon hours there when the place is largely empty. Grace had a little thing going there with Waukonda, a night bartender, a woman obsessed with science and playing backgammon on the Internet. She also keeps late hours. The last time I talked with Grace, he looked like he'd been keeping a few himself. Liz said he looked the same to her that morning when he pulled up in front of the house.

She describes the long drives to the local mill south of town by the river, nerve rattling efforts over narrow rutted back roads that were about to begin. Tough, dangerous work. I'd never met a logger who didn't have scars all over his body including some on the face when a chain had snapped while felling a tree or bucking the limbs. A guy I used to know was killed when his saw ignited a pocket of gas caused by rotting inner wood in an old tree. The explosion sent a large shaft of knotty pine through his throat. Losing a hand, a foot or a few teeth is part of the game. Loggers make hockey players look like game show contestants; they're brutally tough, often crazy and the ones with all their limbs play a mean brand of hockey. Anybody who's worked in the woods for even a few years has the war wounds to prove it. Loggers die every year from falling limbs called "widow makers," from trees that snap back in the sawyer's face, or from machines gone haywire. Long days that too often lead to short careers and permanent disability. I'll take my chances as a PI and a writer.

Liz returned to her work as a free-lance writer (we are a plague visited on the state and Biederbeck in particular) reassured that some money would be coming in soon from Sam's work. Not hers. No one ever pays writers on time or very much, but we both catch ourselves before we stagger down that pathetic conversational path. She actually laughs a little at the insanity of trying to make money writing and adds "But at least we have the respect of the community." Respect is high on a writer's list of priorities. I walk over to the fridge for a can of Schmidt. There are a bunch of them scattered about inside. I grab one with a snarling musky on its label and pop the top. Foam and spray shoot all over my shirt and face. Must have dropped these babies on the way in late one night.

"Cool, calm and collected, that's your style isn't it Bouchee," and I notice her smile. A nice improvement. She is a very pretty woman. "I've heard that you're the class of the town." More laughter. "Actually everyone says you're a good guy who always has time to help. Old-time Montana. I like that."

"Style is a function of breeding and quality living," I say. "Mom provided the genetic end. The quality living part of the equation eludes me."

I have an urge for a smoke, but pass on trying to light another one. One joke at a time here.

She watches me work on the beer, then continues her story. With Sam's income she will be able to answer the phone without hearing the voice of a surly, sub-normal bill collector on the other end of the line. We apparently both share a love for these tireless souls who toil in the collection business.

The next time Liz sees Sam is a couple of weeks later. She can not believe the change. His eyes are starting to bulge from their sockets and, aside from being bloodshot, they have a glazed and yellowish cast to them. Like he has jaundice. He seems to have lost a lot of weight. His jeans hang down on his hips. She can see his ribs pushing through the dirty T-shirt he's wearing. He speaks rapidly in staccato bursts of words with a strained, rough voice that Liz attempts to mimic for me.

"Something's not right up there. Bear sign. Huge piles of scat all over the site. Tracks. Big. Claw marks. In trees. On the Cat. Sounds. Loud. Growls. Barks. Grunts. All night."

"That bad, Liz?"

"Worse and he reeked of whiskey and cigars."

She tells how Sam grabs a bottle of Old Crow from the cupboard over the sink and takes a long pull, wiping his chin and lips on his arm.

"In the morning, when it finally comes. Marks. Lots. No goddamned bears. No. Haven't seen one. They're there though," and more whiskey. " Know it. Grace's gone. At least the bastard left the Cat so I can finish the job. Only six loads to the mill. Mark went to pieces."

"Is that what he really said, 'went to pieces?'" I ask and pull another beer from the refrigerator. I use to drink a lot, now I only drink quite a bit. The new me. "Considering how Grace ended up, that's a curious choice of words."

"Yes," said Liz and she cries some more. I get her a Schmidt. "Pretty sick isn't it. The two of them have been friends since grade school. I just can't imagine either one of them hurting the other. No way. And not ... Oh, shit ... carved up the way he was," and she cries again. I try to help by patting her on the shoulder. This soothes her a touch. She collects herself and continues with the story.

By now Sam is halfway through the Old Crow and pacing back and forth across the kitchen leaving tracks of dried mud on the floor. One hand shakes slightly as it rolls a cigar along the table as though the extremity has a its own life. The other clutches the neck of the whiskey bottle in a white-knuckled grip. Liz attempts to get more details from him but the whiskey kicks in. He staggers off to bed and sleeps through the night. In the morning he gives her a check from the Beiderbeck Lumber Products before heading out the door, dismissing the previous night's ravings as just tiredness and the booze. He says that he'll be back in a week and thinks that he can finish cutting the 47 acres by the first part of August.

Liz sees Sam one week later, the inconsistency of his arrivals no big deal. He has little sense of time. He never has. Works gets done when it's supposed to and he usually shows up within thirty minutes of any given appointment. All in all, a little better than par for the course in this state, where long-time residents move to their own internal clocks and individualistic designs. He can take care of himself. Lots of times he shows up when he shows up. She's used to this after a dozen years of marriage. Except this time he is dead drunk. Clothes filthy. Eyes completely glazed over now. Hair muddy and matted. Skin stretched tightly over the bones of his face. No one has seen Mark around Biederbeck, anywhere else, in weeks. But then a lot of people just come and go as they please around here, so nobody is concerned about his absence. He'll appear up sooner or later, probably drunk from a week-long run with one of his lady friends in Billings or maybe the lead singer, Margot something, from that Canadian rock group he always listens to. Mark's considered handsome by the ladies and he's always had a weakness for them. So a pretty face, bright smile, nice figure, a little small talk over drinks and it's see you later, Grace. Been that way since high school. And nobody really meddles in anyone else's business around here. Interested. Sure, but meddled? No.

Her voice wavers when she tells me about meeting Sam out in the road leading to their house, about the bullet holes in the windshield and back window of the truck's cab. She is crying again, softly this time. Her face radiates pain, sorrow, stuff that flashes across the desk and washes over me in a rush of misery that hits me with weight that sags my shoulders and pushes me down low in my chair. Sam is incoherent, babbling about weird noises in the night. Howls during the day. A chainsaw stuck twenty feet up a tree. Gunfire. A rifle submerged in the creek. Bright, spinning lights floating through the trees.

Liz finally gets Sam in bed with the aid of some more bourbon, a few sleeping pills and a shower that is more balancing act than cleansing experience. While he sleeps the next morning, she drives into Biederbeck and files a report with the police, but they say that the story doesn't "add up," and there isn't "a damn thing to investigate at this point." The cops, especially Jim Qualls, are fair minded, professional and over worked, but they've seen it all and then some many times over, so sometimes they are a bit slow on the uptake. And they are way under gunned. Eleven deputies for 4,000 residents. Long shifts. Few days off. When I said that they think everyone is crazy, I meant it. They do, especially after constantly dealing with drug-blown teens, alcohol-sodden domestic disputes, car wrecks that defy explanation, drunken brawls. All of this tends to make a cop cynical. Liz adds that they checked out the wounded pickup with what she called "aloof cop professionalism," finding a shotgun slug embedded in a round of wood lying in the bed. A chainsaw with a badly bent bar, a large collection of beer cans and bottles, and a half dozen empty whiskey bottles were also scattered in the back. The story was tossed off with "cop disdain" Liz said with a defeated shrug of her shoulders. Just another drunk logger causing trouble in the woods. Better there than on Main Street. The whole scene was "replete with condescending uniformed attitude and general intolerance '"Don't bother us with this crap again, Lady,'" she adds. I find this more than a bit extreme based on my experience with Qualls and his deputies. They are good guys. Hard working. Well trained. So I attribute Liz's negative to the present circumstances. Understandable. Next She drives home. Sam's awake, dressed and doing a slow dance with the whiskey one more time. Questions about what is going on draw evasive, often frenzied replies.

The way Liz has it figured, someone is trying to run Sam and Grace off the sale. Maybe one of the area's more active "Save the Woods" whackos. Several of them have dumped sugar and grinding compound in the gas tanks of machinery at logging operations located on slopes of the Norton, Buffalos and Weirs over the past few months, lunching the engines of some pretty pricey equipment. A couple of the groups, including Wilderness Only Protects (this leads to a curious acronym - WOP), claimed responsibility for this and the fiery destruction of a pair of helicopters used for seismic exploration of potential oil fields. They also are pounding spikes into trees located in the suitable timber base of the national forest of the region. One logger lost an eye when his saw hit one of these, breaking the chain that snapped back into his face. The logging machinery and the helicopters I can understand, even appreciate, but maiming and possibly killing someone for a cause strikes me as cowardly terrorism that only weakens any arguments for saving the remaining good country in Montana. Whatever. I have to think that trying to drive a couple of small time loggers nuts with an illusory grizzly is a bit beyond the limited creativity of WOP or their brethren. A little too imaginative for that crew.

Liz admits that her husband is a hard drinker, pounding down many bottles of Old Crow over the long haul, but she adds that he always drinks for a fun time, usually until he passes out. I've some experience in this area and can fully appreciate some of the arcane nuances of the sport. A "fun time" and "passing out" border on being mutually exclusive even in this town. She says that he's never been violent or over the edge before, but he's both now. Maybe Sam's gone round the bend and become not only a concern, but a menace, to family, friends, innocent bystanders and himself.

Another check from the Biederbeck lumber mill is on the kitchen table, muddy and crumpled, and for only two loads of logs. At least they're caught up with the bills and even a little ahead. I try to imagine what that would be like, but am unable to form any clear image of fiscal solvency. Concepts like 401Ks and health insurance elude me. Not owing anyone money is a vision beyond my sight. Sam carries on with fervor about the grizzly that he is positive is lurking around the site, and about the weird lights and now gunfire, all this while watching a preseason football game between the Bears and Arizona – talk about twisted – two of the lamest franchises in the NFL. Liz said that he looked like what she imagined a raving lunatic might resemble high plains style. Crazed eyes. Face contorted into an angry, menacing expression. Extravagant gesticulations. Ragged jeans. Worn plaid shirt. Scuffed steel-toed work boots. After an hour of arguing about the drinking, Sam's disgust with how badly the Bears are playing, and somehow relating this to the state of the logging industry, equating a "pint-sized, dip-shit quarterback" with the president of the local mill and also with that "pin-head liar from Texas who ran the country," finally subsides. She manages to guide him back to bed. A new sport in the making. She decides that she will find help from somewhere first thing in the morning.

That opportunity never materializes.

Sam disappears in the pickup sometime in the night. She never hears him leave. She sleeps the sleep of the dead from exhaustion brought on from dealing with him and from worry. By now she is past frantic and the Biederbeck cops can't help. Qualls is still out of town. He's delivering a vagrant they'd arrested earlier in the week back to Beloit, Wisconsin where he was wanted for numerous violations of The Mann Act and for shooting up the newsroom at the town's newspaper after they refused to run a Letter to the Editor he'd written about the purported evils of rock music. Just another happy soul riding the Turbid Springs Express, Midwestern style. The deputy in charge, George Mitterwald, said there was nothing to be done (a fairly common and understandable response considering what was known at the time). Sam wasn't a missing person. Nor was Grace. Neither of them had broken any laws with the possible exception of open container violations and speeding. No big deal out here. Besides Mitterwald had his hands full with two drunks who tried to wreck the bowling alley with golf clubs. Tough place. The vast social implications of this heinous deed, how the closure of the facility might affect a large portion of the community, are unimaginable. More of the same from the state police. Tourist season and they're busy sorting the remains of visitors scattered along the interstates, vehicles mangled, as they violently succumb to the thrills of driving over one-hundred miles-per-hour on the wide-open interstate. One way to cull the herd, I guess.

Liz then speaks with the head of the town's alcohol and drug abuse center. He advises her to bring Sam in for a talk aimed at voluntary commitment to an in-patient treatment program, possibly in Minnesota. A four-week stay that might put her husband on the path to recovery. And it only costs seven grand. Liz says that she thought at the time that this was "quite a bargain," especially considering the fact that Sam would never buy into any of the dogma, but at least it was an option. The counselor also mentions that an intervention might be necessary if her husband won't come in on his own. Liz turns this down immediately. Having his friends and his wife commit him, will destroy what faith Sam still has regarding people. Writers. Loggers. Health insurance. They rarely go together and they don't have the cash, so instead, Liz decides to drive up to Indian Creek the next day and see for herself what is going down up there. She'll try and bring Sam back if she can. The hell with the money from the sale. She loves the guy and will do anything to help him. The bills can wait. They always have in the past.

After packing a picnic lunch of ham sandwiches, chips, apples and beer for tomorrow afternoon, Liz goes to bed early. It's barely 8:30. Her last thoughts before drifting off are of Sam and Indian Creek. Then comes the nightmare. In dreams nothing is sacred and everything has an electric, too-sharply-focused quality tinged with bright softness around the edges. She knows she's sleeping but can not wake up or control the stream of images. The dirt road floats beneath her feet as though she is flying. One of those. Drifting beneath the Ponderosa she sees the water of the creek sparkling and making sounds like glass wind chimes. Huge brown trout and Yellowstone cutthroat make high, lazy arcs above the water as they soar thirty, forty feet leaving trails of silver spray in their wakes. Coming through a dense stand of pines she breaks out into the clearing where she sees the raw earth and fresh cut stumps from the logging. Sam is in the middle of the site staring at a chainsaw impaled midway up an old tree, the machine coughing and belching blue smoke. Just below this was a grizzly. The largest she's ever seen, clawing at the saw with human hands. Sunlight flashes off a ring on one hand, the light reflecting bright sapphire blue. While she watches, Sam lifts slowly from the ground until he is opposite the bear. Then the two of them join hands and silently float off above the trees towards the distant peaks of the Nortons. She tries to follow, but keeps tripping over debris, finally stumbling face first into the creek. A large cutthroat leaps over her into the sky. Looking upstream to a small cascade that pours between a pair of boulders she spots Sam standing waist deep in the water trying to pull a large streamer from a bloody wound in his neck. She struggles against the icy current to reach him, but gains none of the distance between them. Her husband's eyes stare at her with glass-dead intensity. She notices that silvery scales have replaced the wet jeans on his lower legs. Fins are forming on the backs of his calves. His silent screams for help and mercy echo in her head.

"I sat up in bed as a man in this awful dream steps from the trees, leers at me, then shoves a long, thin-bladed knife in Sam's stomach," says Liz, face ashen. She drains her beer. "Good God. A little of that type of nonsense goes a long way. The thought of nightmares, any kind, scares the hell out me. I hate to dream. They always seem to come true."

Getting up shakily, she paces back and forth in front of my desk. After waking, she went to the bathroom and splashed cold water on her face. She showers to wash off the sour-smelling sweat that comes from fear. She put on a Blackwatch plaid Pendleton robe, her favorite because Sam gave it to her while they were on a road trip to northern Alberta some years ago. Liz goes to the kitchen, makes strong Ethiopian Harrar coffee and notices that it is

4:30 a.m. A few hours to daybreak. Reading a day-old paper she comes upon a story about a 2,000-pound bull that had fallen off a cliff and landed on a 71-one-year-old woman's Cadillac Seville, obliterating the windshield and breaking the poor lady's arms. Interviewed at the hospital after the incident all she could say was "It was a lot of bull and a lot of shattered glass."

"After everything that had happened over the past few weeks, I cracked up and laughed like a maniac, forever. Think of it. 'It was a lot of bull,'" Liz laughed. "I knew all about that."

I had to laugh, too. It was funny and the fact that Liz could laugh under these circumstances about anything told me a lot about her. Tough. Someone who'd experienced a lot of life and had not turned cold and hard in the process. I already find myself admiring her courage, determination and, I guess I can say, her style, for lack of any other word. Our merriment wakes the dog, who immediately realizes that it is too early for his show. He circles on the couch three times, collapses in a furry heap and goes back to sleep with a deep sigh that seems to acknowledge how hard all our lives, and in particular his, are sometimes. Springers. They're hopeless.

Liz says that she felt better with the light of sunrise. She starts her old Toyota Landcruiser, a solid rig that she had purchased from an old hipster in Missoula back in the early seventies. The ride is a bit rough, but the thing always starts and never breaks down. Liz places the picnic basket on the seat beside her and a cooler filled with beer and ice on the floor.

"Well, Ed, I thought 'What the hell? Nothing like a

breakfast beer.' And it tasted very good and felt great in my stomach."

This made me thirsty, so I raided the fridge one more time, finding a couple of Nut Brown Ales from a small Whitefish Brewery. A friend of mine makes the stuff and a meager living along with it. In return for my promise to mention his product at every chance, he keeps me in beer. Fair deal. Tidrow now serves it at Ray's. The bottles foam darkly when I pry off the caps. Liz takes a long hit and says "Not bad."

She recalls the drive with almost lyrical enthusiasm. After awhile she turns off the highway and starts in on the Indian Creek Road, dodging rocks, ruts and bumps. The affair is one of the Forest Service's finer efforts, a bouncing little thing that leads deep into mostly timbered country filled with streams, beaver ponds and mountain cirque lakes of pure, ice-cold water and lots of trout. The Dog and I have spent many days camping in there catching fish and hanging around camp. It's country that buzzes with an untamed hum. By this time Liz sees that the sun is well up and the trees glisten from an early-season frost and from melted water. The creek shimmers in the crystal light under a cloudless, blue sky. Large, cleaned patches of gravel can already be seen along the streambed – redds, or spawning nests, made by male cutthroat trout for laying their eggs. The females had deposited their eggs in these areas recently being spring to early-summer spawners. She also spots several males holding in shadowy patches of the stream a few feet below the redds. Cutthroat are rising to caddis and mayflies all over the place. She brakes hard for five whitetails. The first four bound across the road, but the fifth is a thinker, looking this way and that before finally opting for the company of his peers, prancing with dainty strides across the road, and pausing to look directly at Liz before the animals disappear into the forest. After an hour of driving, thinking and sipping beer, she sees the logging site a couple of miles ahead off below her as she rounds a narrow high curve that also revealed several 11,000-foot peaks of the Nortons, the tops covered with the remains of last winter's snow. Deer are here, also. Big game season is still months away and the animals are everywhere. Standing in the trees, in open meadows, crossing the road. She spots a large elk grazing in a clearing high above. An eagle soars overhead riding the thermals and a pair of Red-tailed hawks cruise low over an open ridge. The work site is far from any homes. The few people that live in this remote part of Montana are located back down in the foothills close to the highway. Liz stops on the side of the road and gets out of the car. The first thing she notices is that the skid-cat is wedged up against a Ponderosa. Brush and dried mud cover its treads. The exhaust stack is bent at a ninety-degree angle, the seat torn out, chunks of foam from the cushion scattered about, wires and belts ripped from their connections, and wheels and the faded yellow body paint is scarred by what looked like claw marks. Drops of diesel fuel leak from a torn line and puddle darkly on the hard, dry ground.

Liz said that fear, feeling "like chunks of sharp ice," stabbed her insides, feeling nothing like this morning's beer.

Most of the trees in the area are felled, limbed and stacked in piles ready to be hauled to the mill. Here and there a tree lies on the ground, stump splintered. No sign of Sam, but unmistakable, in the middle of the clearcut, is the tree from her dream. A chainsaw, bar twisted and bent, is jammed in the pine well above the reach of any human. Liz almost panics and runs, but forces herself to approach the tree. Her vision is shaky and blurred, but she has no doubt about the deep rips in the bark. Claw marks. Nearby is a mound of earth. She hears a muffled sob from the creek. Following a trail of beer and whiskey bottles, along with cigar butts, she finds Sam slouched on a boulder in the middle of the creek, feet dangling in the water. He is nothing but skin and bones, blue-toned emaciation, face contorted into a death mask. Lifeless. Hideous. Clutched in one hand is an empty bottle of Beam. In the other is a dead brown trout. The Mossberg is on the bank, barrel twisted like the chainsaw bar.

"So much for the picnic," Liz says and looks at me with eyes that have seen maybe too much of what life can be. The last couple of months have obviously been difficult for her. She tries to smile again and it sort of works. The old gallows humor two-step. I appreciate the effort and the fact that she is obviously stronger than she looks which is pretty tough to begin. The best ones always are and they always seem to be married. Even if all of the quality women aren't married, it's hard for me to visualize any of them sharing their lives with a PI slash writer slash fly fishing fanatic with, at best, a slight chance of striking it rich or acquiring anything even approximating wealth. I often get discouraged and wonder if people ever get married because they are in love with each other. One can dream, though I've pretty much accepted the fact that it's down to The Dog, myself and my friends. If wealth is having loyal, funny, good people for friends, then I'm way beyond being a multi-millionaire. Dirt, The Count, Jim Qualls, and on and on. I'm a lucky soul in this respect and many others, like living in this outrageous corner of the world and having good health. It easy to complain and I often do, but I'm happy with my life. But back to Liz and her story.

"I yelled 'Sam. Sam!' but he didn't recognize me," she says and then takes a sip of beer and pulls a cigarette from my pack on the desk. She selects a stick match from the half-open red and blue box, and lights the smoke, that instantly bursts into a small blaze. Inhaling deeply, she blows long clouds of smoke from her nose. "How old are these? Stale doesn't quite get it. As Twain said, 'Quitting's easy. I've done it a hundred times,' but I enjoy these horrible things so much."

She continues smoking for a minute then continues. "I yelled as loud as I could 'Sam!' and this time his head turns very slowly, rotating like some perverted mechanical doll. The eyes are vacant, fogged over. Not Sam's anymore. I used to love looking into them whenever I could, but not these. They were ghastly, like something from a Wes Craven movie character. The worst face I've ever seen. It hurt and terrified me all at once.

"'Come meet Brownie. She's a fine old wench,' Sam croaks in a voice that is not his. This one has a weak, whining, distant, sick tone. Perverted. 'Brownie. My sweet Brownie.'"

She then describes how she steps into the stream, the cold chilling her legs, and reaching what has become of her husband. This takes only a few seconds that seem like the eternity of a wicked dream.

"I don't remember the drive back or taking Sam to the emergency room. I was really out of it. I can't remember one thing about that drive, even today. Only the fear and the sick feeling and dizziness."

I light another Camel, this time without incident and look over some notes I've made. "How's Sam doing now?"

"I called the police from the hospital and told them what I'd found and they went right up. Qualls said they found Mark's grave in a matter of minutes. Actually, after talking with you, I see now that he's a good guy and helping all he can. This has been good for me. Thank you," and she smiles a little again. "It was that fresh mound of dirt I saw. He said they put Sam under arrest in his room immediately. That he was the logical, and for now, only suspect. And that considering his present condition, this works for his own protection as much as anything. "

I agree with Qualls' assessment and actions. This seems to calm her even more. Progress, slight though it may be is welcome.

"A couple of day's after finding Mark's body, when Sam was healthy enough for the ride, they shipped him off to Turbid Springs for tests and evaluation," she says. "He could be there for years the way Lynn is handling things. Damn! That man is worse than useless. All he cares about is his public image and getting re-elected. I saw Sam yesterday and he is obsessed with someone named 'Brownie.' He sure doesn't recognize me.

"They've got him eating regularly again and he's not that hideous blue-white color, but he's not Sam anymore, either." That brings some tears, but again quickly regains her composure.

"I don't know what to say," I say and mean it. "I hear some strange stories in this work, but your troubles give new meaning to the words 'curious' and 'twisted.' Were there any signs of another person or vehicle? Boot tracks or tire marks? Anything?

She turns her head slightly and looks out the window onto Main for a moment. Something bothers me about this, frightens me some. I'm not sure if I should take on the case. The story is weird enough, but I have the feeling Liz is holding back even stranger stuff, that she wants me, hell anyone, to help so that she doesn't feel so alone, isolated, but she's afraid that opening up completely will scare me off. She may be right, but she needs help. The murder is dark enough, but I feel a current of something truly bad, pure distilled essence of evil running through all of this. I sense this from the queasiness in the pit of my stomach and tightened my chest. More importantly I seem to see the slightest of dark glimmerings on the far edges of my vision. When I turn my head to catch what these are, all I see is more of my office. An unsettling and unfamiliar experience. What radar I have says in large red words across my brain "Run like hell from this one." I never have listened to this in the past much to my chagrin, to put things mildly. I figure 'Why start now?' The money will help. It always does. And I really do already like her to the point of wanting to help. Her courage, her stamina are impressive, but the craziness and violence. Second thoughts zip around all over the place. Maybe that's what I'm seeing on the fringes of things.

"I did see some marks on the bank, like footprints from waders, but they could have been Sam's, though at this time of the year he prefers to wade wet in just jeans and tennis shoes. He always enjoys wearing an old pair of Converse All Stars that have felt soles he's cut and glued to the bottoms. Better than spending two hundred bucks for pricey wading boots, he often said. And he never goes anywhere without a couple of flyrods and boxes of flies. He loves to fish. So, other than those tracks, nothing, I guess."

"And Qualls is convinced Sam murdered Grace? They're not looking in any other directions?"

"No. They think he went off the deep end with the booze. They've chalked the whole thing up to a drunken, nut case who killed his business partner and best friend. Who can really blame them. If I were investigating this, I'd have a damn hard time even considering the possibility that anyone but Sam killed Mark. But I know he's innocent. I have no doubts what so ever. Forget my love for him. Forget all of that. Please believe me, because tell you that my instincts say someone else did this."

"I think I do, though I know little right now, but Qualls' reaction is understandable under the circumstances," I say. "Looks like an easy one to solve and they may be right. Sam may have lost it. Booze has knocked out a few of my friends over the years. Came close to finishing me off until a woman friend of mine made me look at some things differently and nursed me through the withdrawal, which was total hell, but let's move on."

Liz looks at me with kindness, understanding that feels like she's been there. Then the slight smile surfaces quickly like a rising rainbow after mayflies on a summer's evening along a deep bank of the river near town.

"I'll check around a little bit. Make some calls. See what I can find out. I'll charge you for the time and expenses. A couple of hundred, perhaps three hundred bucks at the most."

"You'll help. Thanks. Thank you," she says. "You have no idea how this makes me feel. I'm not alone in this anymore. We're going to clear Sam. Yes. Go ahead and do it. I have a little money put away. Yes. Do it! I can't stand not knowing, not having Sam around anymore. Being alone. I'm worn out."

Then she cries a lot this time. Once again I'm not much of a comforting force, but she pulls it together one more time, thanks me and leaves. I see her drive off down Main in the Landcruiser that trails a slim trail of blue-black exhaust - a ring job in the offing. Uncovering anything in this bizarre mess will be difficult, especially with the assorted loonies, cult casualties, drug dealers, drifters, grifters and other mendicant atrocities that blow through the area. Montana in the warm months is a Mecca of sorts for the socially inept and or deranged. Worrisome on occasion, but a fact of life that's not all that hard to accept and deal with.

The Dog sits up, shakes his head, jumps off the couch and pushes his way out the door. It's that wonderful time of day when he begs for food from the usual suspects of business owners along the street and introduces himself wet-nose-style to a few of the tourists that work the streets when they're not down south an hour or so from Biederbeck playing bumper cars or wilderness gridlock on the narrow roads in Yellowstone Park. The Dog's afternoon sojourn always seems to be good for a few canine laughs, cheap thrills and too much food. His weakness is Almond Joys. He loves coconut and like a true addict, denies that chocolate is bad for him. A lot of people know about his addiction and like pushers the world over they feed his habit. Every day is a form of Halloween for the little guy. I watch as he looks up and down Main, checking for driftboats, no doubt. Ever since the mayhem at Red Head's Trap he keeps his piece of the wreckage next to him on the couch. If he spots a driftboat parked on the street, he'll run home or if he sees one passing by from his perch on the couch as he gazes through the window as the craft is being towed to or from the river, he'll grab his totem, jump to the floor and hide in the closet, often for more than an hour. I wonder if he'd ever go fishing with Dirt and me again. On his uptown wanderings, his favorite place is the dumpster in the alley behind Ray's, especially on Sunday morning after the prime rib special on Saturday night. He often returns with a distended belly and a large end piece of beef clutched in his jaws. He is famous for this behavior in town. The Dog is as easily amused as I am, though I haven't resorted to dumpster diving, yet. Returning to my desk and the smoldering remains of a cigarette, I ponder Liz's troubles. A real nice lady with some big problems and secrets. A strange deal. Very strange indeed.

~ ~ ~

The wind is roaring hard and cold as it piles down off the Rocky Mountain Front, slicing through the sheer, grey rock canyons where Deep Creek and Two Medicine River join. Looking back up either drainage, narrow views of the mountains reveal themselves briefly between twisting masses of purple and black clouds. Harsh white sheets of snow and ice slash straight down from the ridges, then are ripped sideways in the compressed gale piling through the gorges. By late October the weather has turned in the direction of winter driving elk to forested cover down low and sweeping the air clear of hawks and eagles. Sharp-tailed grouse hold tight beneath tight clumps of chokecherry and alder growing in the protection of tight, curling draws. Cutthroat trout swim along the bottoms of deep pools, down where things are quiet. Trees, bushes and grass buck violently with the force of the onslaught. Snow rarely accumulates this early in the season. What does fall is swiftly blown eastward over the dead, brown grasses of the high plains, that are now streaked with sheets of brittle sunlight that rakes the ground through rips in the overcast.

A banged up, rusted-out, brown pickup carrying two men lurches across a rocky bluff above the streams. Progress is slow, but they steadily closed ground on what remains of the Sisika (or Black Foot) Indians' buffalo herd that wanders without purpose in nearly total isolation beneath the mountains in northwest Montana. The tribe has spent years and many thousands of dollars trying to return the animals to their native range on the reservation, trucking forty of the animals south a decade ago from grazing lands just over the border in Alberta, Canada. They'd purchased the bison from a related tribe called Akainawa (or Bloods). These animals had been culled from the northern herd, an annual process needed to keep the bison numbers at level equal or below the carrying capacity of the land. Instead of slaughtering all of the excess animals for meat, robes and other uses, the Akainawa agreed to sell the bison to their Montana counterparts in hopes of making a small stride towards re-establishing the species on the northern high plains. Probably a futile attempt, but a noble gesture all the same. When the animals arrived, the Sisika prayed and fasted in hopes that these buffalo would be the start of something grander, perhaps even a living spiritual tie to their proud free-ranging past. In the first years the herd had grown to almost one-hundred and fifty, and given a fair chance, could have passed a thousand. But when the tribal council begin to think that the operation was on the up-and-up and running smoothly, when the members had bought into the visual and verbal dog-and-pony show, the man who managed the herd was running down, this so-called manager and his cohorts made their move. They were non-tribal individuals with no concern for the Sisika, their plight or their history. Money was all they cared about. Now, six years later, less than forty animals remain, thirty-seven to be exact. No one ever checks anymore and the manager conjures enough excuses, explanations and lies involving brucellosis, predation from mountain lions, grizzlies and wolves, harsh weather and poaching by tribal members to keep the trust of the council. They all believe that he's a hard-working, dedicated man who has the best interests of The People at heart. They are a bit wrong on this one and in a not so indirect way the tribe's heritage suffers.

Buffalo, or bison if the need to be correct is overpowering, have always been an integral part of the tribe's way of living. Yearly rhythms in a large part revolved around the movements of the buffalo herds that often consisted of millions of animals. In the past the Sisika relied on this abundance of the buffalo and the animals' many utilitarian aspects to sustain them. The animals yielded meat and other forms of nutrition. The tribe relished the cheese-like contents of the intestines of newborn calves. Buffalo fat and berries mixed with the animals' blood was a favorite dessert at feasts. Functional uses included hides for lodges, robes, lacings, ropes, moccasins, mittens and caps. Spoons and cups were crafted from the horns, water buckets from the paunch. The scrotum of a bull made a durable stirrup cover and they made glue from a bull's phallus by slicing the member into small pieces and boiled, and so on. In short, buffalo were life to these people and as a result many tales evolved concerning the buffalo and its role in Siska living.

One of these stories tells of four tribal members who went to war with their brothers against the Cree. The journey was long and tough and they became separated from the main group in the course of the running battle. Distance and severe terrain finally finished in their horses, who dropped soaked in lathered sweat, foam dripping from their mouths. So they began the arduous return trip on foot, tired, thirsty and emotionally spent. Eventually they came to the Sand Hills in Saskatchewan. Essentially they were in the middle of nowhere, many days ride from home. The country drifted off far beyond the horizon in all directions. Dry washes and large coulees that cut through the land made travel difficult. Loose salmon and ochre shaded soil and rocks gave way beneath their feet. Snakes hissed at them as they stumbled by. Coyotes laughed at their futile efforts. While passing through this desolate, unpopulated country they spotted a fresh travois trail. One of the men said, "This is hopeless. We're as good as dead. We might as well follow this trail. Perhaps we'll come up with some of our people. Dead is dead, so let's give this a shot. What have we got to lose," or something along those lines. They followed the trail for many miles when finally one of their number uttered in abject exhaustion "Why follow this any longer? It is just nothing. This is bullshit," or, once again, something along those lines. The others replied, "Not so. These are our people that have left these tracks. We will go camp with them." They continued for hours. Then in the silence and orange glow of sunset one of them discovered a stone maul and a dog travois lying in the native grasses. He said, "Look at these things. I know this maul and this travois. They belonged to my mother, who died. They were buried with her." With a look of "if this gets any weirder I'm going to lose my mind," he cautiously picked up the possessions to bring back home. When night set upon them they camped in a shelter offered by a copse of trees. A small spring bubbled up from the ground and poured over bright emerald and lilac-hued mosses. They built a large fire from deadfall. The blaze warmed them and helped ease their fears and awesome loneliness. They'd killed a small whitetail deer earlier in the day that they hastily cooked over the fire. They devoured the hot, singed meat, bloody juices running down their chins and dripping from their hands. They laughed at their own savagery and let out wild, slightly mad cries that sailed out to the stars. Packs of coyotes roaming the surrounding grasslands hunting rabbits and small, careless rodents howled back in reply, mimicking the sounds of the Those-Who-Stand-Alone braves. The men wailed back in unrestrained response and the packs replied adding a riff of their own. The free-form music splashed across the night and the braves lost their fear and regained their touch with the land, with who they were.

When they awoke early in the morning they heard all about them sounds as if a camp of people were there. They heard a young brave shouting a war cry, women chopping wood, and a man calling for a feast. Dogs barked and yipped. The four Sisika looked in every direction but could see nothing. Only the familiar sounds of their brothers rode the airwaves around them. Frightened, they covered their heads with buffalo robes, but finally summoned the courage to look about once more. They saw nothing but wild, empty land at first. Then one of them shouted, "Look over there. See that pis'kun (a narrowing structure that herds buffalo either over a cliff where they plunge to their deaths or into a confined area where they can be readily killed). Let's go over and look at it. While approaching the pis'kun, one of the braves picked up a stone-pointed arrow and exclaimed "Look at this. It belonged to my father. This is his work. His way of chipping rock to make a killing point. This is the place." And then as they advanced the pis'kun suddenly vanished. A little while after this one of them yelled "Look over there. There is my father running buffalo. There! He has killed one," as the hunter in the vision plunged his spear through the heart of the galloping beast, which immediately collapsed, front legs buckling, head and horns pile driving into the dirt.. "Let us go over with him." They all could now see a man on a white horse running buffalo across the vast prairie. They ran towards the man who had killed the large bull and saw him drop from his horse to view his kill. He was a tall man who wore moccasins that laced to his knees. His long, black braids swung below his waist. Red, yellow and white pigments slashed across his prominent cheekbones. He looked over at the four and his eyes flashed with a powerful blaze. Then he threw his head back and howled, before beckoning the braves to him with a slow gesture from a long, muscular arm. They started to approach, but before they reached the kill, the man got on his horse and rode away over the far horizon, screaming with the wind. Where the slain buffalo had been, they found only a dead mouse. By the side of the mouse was a buffalo chip and lying on it was an arrow painted red. The man said, "That was my father's arrow. That is the way he painted them." He took it in his hands and immediately saw that it was nothing but a blade of grass. When he laid it down it was an arrow again. Another of their group located a buffalo stone which is the fossil of a small prehistoric animal. The four looked at each other in confusion and terror. All of them were shaking as though very cold despite their efforts to remain calm and brave. In near panic, they rode the strange energy of this fear home, using the power in this unknown force to carry their feet over hundreds of miles of rough trail, through storms filled with gale-driven rain and sleet, and on over interminable, white-hot, alkali flats where large flies tormented them and took pieces of there scalps and face with burning, tearing bites. Again, snakes coiled in piles of scorched rock hissed in derision as they passed, but that terror of the unexplained visions drove then onward and one day near dark they spotted the lodges of their village. They were back among their people, but changed from their journey. Life was different for all of them now.

Some time after returning home the man who had taken the maul and dog travois breathed smoke from a fire and died coughing and clutching his throat, his face turning purple black. His horse died the same way the next morning. The Sisika believed that the shadow of the person who owned these objects was angry with him for some reason, followed the brave home and killed him in vengeance. Two of the others died horribly in battle, their bodies left scalped, mutilated and rotting beneath the sun, torn apart and devoured by vultures and coyotes, and the biting flies. The one who found his father's stone and arrow point, took them wherever he went. He lived a long life. Though badly wounded in two fights, he survived his injuries, miraculously healed. His father's possessions were his medicine. Arrows through his lungs, a knife wound to the neck, two legs broken when his horse was shot out from under him - he survived all of this and grew stronger in spirit each day. As for the one who took the buffalo rock, he was now able to call in large numbers of the animals for his people. He would pray over the rock while sitting next to his lodge fire, chanting far into the night. His eyes took on a distant, visionary, lonesome cast. He was not shunned by his people. They respected him, but when he spoke it was with words in a language they could not fathom. He was still one of the tribe, but he was no longer of their world. His was now the life of the seekers, one of power and isolation. When he would ask for a hundred buffalo to jump into the pis'kun, the next day one hundred would jump in. His connection to what most saw as the unknown fed his people. That was his isolating, frightening gift.

Such is the nature of belief and power. Such was The People's way of life in this country.

What does any of this lore have to do with the two men who ride in the battered truck? Perhaps nothing right now. Perhaps a good bit of everything sometime later.

The white man in charge of the herd, Bill Hands, recently told the tribal council that there are now 100 buffalo. A stone cold lie. Remember, there are less than the original forty. The council, essentially a political body which behaves as political bodies normally do, smiled and nodded its approval, unaware of the real situation, not really caring as long as they hear the right words and are shown the right graphs indicating a steady growth in animal numbers. This council has several members who are on the take from various private concerns such as a booking agency located in Bozeman that arranges special trips for wealthy fly fishing clients. A few thousand bucks here and there gained exclusive rights for the Bozeman business. Hands strengthened his position with promises of government mineral rights easements on tribal lands, most notably holdings of council members. So, the council is more than happy and satisfied with whatever Hands tells them. No one really knows what is going on with the buffalo. No one has ever checked with any determination or thoroughness. They trust the word of this white man. Of all people, they should have known better, including his riff about mineral rights easements. There is no such action on the horizon. A down-and-out ranch hand with a gift for fast talk and elaborate con, he's managed to win the trust of two council members with swift talk of future wealth and power. The pair gave him the job when the position arose. A little under-the-table cash may have changed hands in this deal, too. Such is the nature of the political scene wherever it plays itself out. Each year the man and a partner, the two who are now bouncing along in the truck, move out to this isolated portion of the Rez where the huge, dark animals graze and breed. They do this in the spring when most of the snow is gone and also in the autumn. Over a period of several days each season they shoot a couple of dozen or more of the buffalo. The number of animals shot initially factored in the keeping of the herd level at 100 animals or so. Greed now carries the day and the numbers are on a fast track to zero. This meat is sold to various fancy restaurants around the country. The men unload the hides and horns to leather workers and boutique craft shops here and there, including one exorbitantly priced artsy emporium in Biederbeck. This is then turned into fancy moccasins, gaudily-beaded belts and buffalo horn cribbage boards. Neat stuff. Some of the animals weigh a ton and at two dollars per pound the two make good money. More than some lawyers, especially when the sale of the hides, horns and various internal organs is factored in.

The animals either graze or stand stock still in the wind. Plains animals evolved over centuries. They are used to heavy weather, and they are also used to the truck. It usually brings oil cake and other food for them. It's been six months since they've last heard gunfire. The stoic animals watch silently as members of their group drop to the ground coughing spumes of blood onto the heartless ground. They've forgotten last spring's shooting.

The truck stops within seventy-five yards of the animals who appear only slightly alarmed as indicated by raised tails and occasional breathy grunts. The man hired by the Sisika to protect and enlarge the herd grabs a rifle and climbs out of the driver's side. He is lean and nearly six feet tall, but he looks small, almost frail compared to the much larger man who exits the other side of the truck. Six-feet-eight, with the body of an NFL linebacker that ran along the lines of Ted "The Mad Stork" Hendricks of the old Oakland Raiders, along with dark, unkempt hair, bushy eyebrows and a close-cropped beard shot through with grey. This individual holds a rifle that looks toy-like in his large hands. He sights through the scope on a large bull and then the pair move closer, eventually winding up standing side by side in the brittle wind. They take aim on the bulls and fire, repeatedly. The buffalo look on the fallen members of the herd with silent curiosity. The men keep shooting and more animals die - bulls and several cows, the calves balling beside their now-dead mothers. Large caliber rifles at this range are coldly efficient. Rounds just behind the shoulder, through the heart and lungs, or higher up breaking necks do the job. The beasts fall with deep, agonized bellows, legs buckling beneath them before they collapse to the frozen earth with leaden thuds. The sound of the gunfire dissipates swiftly in the gale, gun smoke vanishing in an instant.. No talk or exchanged glances. Only rapid, killing gunfire. Within a couple of minutes 13 buffalo are dead or dying in the dry blue grama and buffalo grass. The animals' dark blood pools and coagulates on the surface of the brown soil and amid the clumps of dry grasses. The rest of the herd moves off over the bluff and down to the shelter of the canyons. The buffalo don't stampede in terror. They just wander across the far rise, soon out of sight. Then a semi-tractor-trailer slowly works its way to the killing ground, pulling up next to the dead buffalo. The truck's driver gets out and unloads a fork lift from within. The carcasses are quickly and efficiently scooped up piled inside the trailer. Next the fork lift is reloaded. The job is completed in less than an hour. The two shooters silently smoke cigarettes. They say nothing. One of them walks over to a fallen animal and cuts off the last four inches of its tail, shoving the brushy thing in his coat pocket. In near darkness now, the two rigs drive without lights back to the highway and on down the road to an isolated ranch outside of Dupuyer about an hour to the south. The Reservation is sparsely populated with most of the tribal members living in and around Browning. No one is out this way. No one has witnessed the shooting. Within days the animals will be gutted, butchered, packaged and shipped in trim hunks to a warehouse in Omaha and then on to San Francisco, New York, Atlanta, Chicago, and other cities around the country. No one is aware of any of this and the herd never gets any larger. Cash on the hoof and another Sisika dream up in smoke.

~ ~ ~

Thirteen buffalo carcasses hang from large hooks attached to steel cables bolted to 12-by-12 beams running along the ceiling of the cooler. The meat shows muted red-purple through thin, translucent layers of fat and membrane. The animals glow ghostly and headless beneath the unnatural brightness of the fluorescent lights humming above. The lifeless, metallic smell of blood is pervasive. Out on the cement floor of the barn thirteen large, mangy heads are piled in one corner, dead eyes staring off in the direction of nowhere. All of the heads have already been bought and paid for by an oil company CEO in Houston. They will be mounted at his new hunting lodge under construction in the hill country of west Texas. Pathetic still life reminders of what once was and never will be again, a grizzly sight in the offing. The thick, bloody hides are scattered about like victims of a casual LA fast-food-restaurant slaughter. These will be brain-tanned later, a process that will turn the hides into soft, luxuriant robes. Internal organs such as hearts, livers and gall bladders, along with the bulls' testicles, are already packaged, wrapped and neatly stored in the back of the cooler. They will be shipped to countries along the Pacific Rim, to individuals willing to pay high prices for the parts' curative and restorative properties. Longer life, greater strength, increased sexual performance - the buffalos' body parts hold the false promise of this elusive magic for those living in places like Japan, Korea and China. The last few inches of each of the severed tails lay in a pile on a work bench near the cooler. They resemble Honduran maduro-wrapped double corona cigars. The floor is awash, slippery, in blood and guts from the butchering. The semi's driver is busy sluicing down the mess with a high-pressure hose. The two men who did the shooting stand near the double doors that open out to the ranch yard. They are smoking black cigars that also resemble the bison tail stubs. They share a bottle of whiskey with a third man who's met them here in the dark shortly after they returned from the killing. All of them are experienced with skinning the animals so the work goes quickly. A routine has been established over the past few years. Cut the heads off with a chainsaw. Skin the robes with slick strokes from razor-sharp knives. Slice open the bellies and pull out the guts. Simple, brutal, bloody, and very profitable, work.

The wind has died down and the sky is clear. Uncountable numbers of stars and galaxies blast their blue-white light down through the icy air. It is bright enough out that the barn, ranch house and surrounding cottonwoods cast distinct shadows across the ground and over Sheep Creek running over its cobbled streambed.

The tall, bearded one takes a hit from the bottle, inhales deeply from his cigar and blows out a thick cloud of smoke that hangs in the air, neither rising or sinking to the ground. The stuff just holds there in front of the three men. The one cleaning up the blood finishes the job and walks over to the group, his boots making a wet and brittle sound on the cement. The tall man offers him a cigar, then a flame from a lighter that has a nasty-looking snake – flashing tongue, long, sharp fangs and yellow eyes - etched on its surface. The four smoke and work on the whiskey in silence. Meteors shoot across the sky, coming in from all directions, some so close the men watch as parts of the sizzling chunks of matter break off and fizzle away in tangential directions arcing in sparkling trails of silver and gold. High doings in a natural way along the Rocky

Mountain Front. The men are content, pleased with what they've accomplished in the last twelve hours. Good money is involved here. Well into six figures when the sale of the buffaloes' organs to their new-found distributor in Tacoma is factored in. Far into six figures. And easy money, too.

"Could shoot those dumb shits all day long and skin their hides way through the night," the tall one snarls. "Don't give a lick for those randy savages in the first place. Screwing 'em out of their goddamn sacred mangy cows makes me laugh. Poor excuse for a race. Warriors my ass. Squaws is more like it. Suck government tit for a monthly check and drink it down on cheap-ass wine in two days. Losers. And where the hell have you been? You have a knack for avoiding the bloody work."

"Couldn't be helped. Sam's truck broke down and I had to help him out," says the late arrival, a blond-haired man a few inches shorter than the group's leader, both men in their forties. "You always did have a kind word for the Indians. Chicanos, blacks and Orientals, too, as I remember. I don't have a problem with the easy money we're making, but it bothers some to cheat the tribe this way. They don't have a clue." Light plays off a large blue stone mounted in a ring on the middle finger of the man's right hand. The leader catches sight of the flash and the meanness in him grows larger.

"Serves the dumb bastards right, Grace," he mutters. He grabs the dying whiskey bottle from him and kills it off in one long slug. "Grover, drag your butt over to the truck and grab another bottle of Beam and some of those black Mexican cigars from the dash. Still thirsty and I like my nicotine."

"Sure thing, man," and while Grover plays gopher, the tall man stares hard at Grace before asking in a cold monotone "You going soft on me, Mark old buddy? 'Cause if you are, we're getting things straight now and I plan on making my point on how things are going to be. So, what the hell's it going to be? In or out," and the way he said "out" makes Grace shiver.

"Relax Thomas. I need the money and the other dough we turn on those damn trout down in the Nortons. I've got my share of bills and an ex-wife who won't let me be. I'm all the way in. You know that. I was just saying that sometimes I don't feel right about cheating the Sisikas. They've been hammered by everybody for years. It kind of gets to me now and then."

"Took long enough Grover," and he grabs a bottle from the man's hands, twisting off the cap and draining a quarter of it in one motion. Then he lights one of the cigars, sucks in the smoke to the bottoms of his lings, holds it there for a couple of beats before blowing the smoke at Grace. "Lose that 'I'm so sorry for the poor Indians' shit. It's tough out here and if they can't see it straight, screw 'em. Screw 'em all, the lame idiots," and the man laughs, a heartless sound made all the meaner when accompanied with the dark glow that burns through hooded eyes.

"Jesus! Ease up Thomas. Grace has always done his share. Let's not fuck things up now just when we're starting to make real money," says Grover Loudermilk, whose only claim to fame was acquiring the nickname Slim while hitting .337 with 28 home runs for a Class A minor league team in Appleton, Wisconsin twenty-five years ago, He reaches for the bottle, but their leader decks the man with a left that comes from nowhere in a flash. Grover hits the ground, out cold. The leader pour a splash of whiskey on him, laughing all the while. "Speak that pea-brained shit to my face again you little weasel dick and I'll have you hangin' from a hook with those dead cows. I can see that I'm goin' to have to watch both you clowns from here on out. Soft is the only way jerks like you travel when life turns sporting. Remember, Grace, I'm watchin' real hard now. Hear me?"

Grace nods and says "Yes," quietly.

"Don't try and turn on me and be like those useless jerk-offs up near Yellowstone," he says. "Friends of the Wild Geese they call themselves. All they do is piss and moan about the poor, damn buffalo. If the fools had their way they'd let the animals starve up in the high plateau country. God! They're idiots. The damn buffalo never wintered up there. Jesus. Let 'em starve for all I care. Waste the meat. Used to make a little money shooting and skinning those buffalo. State and Feds paid me pretty well. Enough to keep me in whiskey through the cold times. Damn animal-lover morons who can't see beyond their puny, bleeding hearts. Now they've killed that off for me. Bastards are turning all this into an amusement park for the damned. All the good stuff's gone. You go that direction and I'll rip your guts out on the spot, Grace. Hear me?"

"I'm with you one-hundred percent," says Grace. "The money is important, but I'm hooked on the juice of running this hustle, too. Reminds me of when I was a kid and used to smuggle Molson Ale over the border from

Canada. Beer never tasted so good. I never thought that I'd feel this alive again. I won't let you down."

"That's better," says the leader. "If it's juice you need, I promise you on my soul there's plenty more waiting down the road a piece."

The tall one hands his partner the whiskey and laughs his long, black laugh again, the sound carrying forever on the frigid night air. A pack of coyotes that's been chattering, howling and barking away on bluff overlooking the creek a mile upstream, goes dead silent. The night turns even colder as an icy wind smelling of snow from the Far North begins pouring down from the high peaks of the front. Grover moans. Grace shivers. The tall one smokes his black cigar.

-TWO-

THE WATER BUBBLES AND GLIDES soft and cool along the far bank. It is the first week of August and the tall grass is still bright green. Normally it would be shades of dry brown. It has been a wet year and this is the first time Dirt and I have fished The Hart or any other stream for that matter. The water has been too high to wade and the big fish have been holding out of reach, not actively feeding. The two of us usually fish together every other week or so in warm weather and then into the golden crispness of late October and finally the bleak but rewarding frigid gray monotones of early November. The unusual conditions have altered our behavior, too. Normally the flow in this river gets hammered by irrigation draw down, but this season ranchers are leaving the river alone. They don't need the additional water. In fact, the fields are too wet in some places for them to get their machinery in for the second cutting of hay. So much the better for us now that the river is finally fishing. Instead of holding down deep and skulking around in dark holes like outlaw thugs, eating the occasional stray sculpin or caddis nymph, large, hungry brown trout are up all over the place, holding close to the banks near the surface waiting for breeze-blown grasshoppers to come their way. And this is a banner season for the bulky bugs. We've been fishing for less than an hour and we've already landed a half-dozen trout between eighteen and twenty-two inches. We always release these fantastic fish, but the urge to kill a couple is, while somewhat buried by generations of so-called civilized living, is instinctive and calls strongly at times. We are launching a ragged pattern of Dirt's own design, a tragic combination of sage grouse feathers, antelope hair, rusty gold Antron dubbing and a sprig of red cut from an old flannel shirt of his. The hopper looks like hell, but it works. As Dirt often said, "Artistic flies catch small, cute fish. Big, ratty bugs take big, ugly browns. Take your pick." We both like big, ugly browns.

My friend is casting a beautiful Payne cane rod. A seven-six, four-weight weathered Hardy Perfect reel. Cane isn't as durable as the new high-tech fibers. Nor is it as accurate or strong when it comes to casting. When one of these beautiful aesthetically pleasing wonders explodes, shatters far beyond recognition and repair, the experience is traumatic. I've seen Dirt go silent for days after one of his cherished bamboo rods blows up while bending gracefully against the force and weight of a large, angry brown, but as he said "They are made to be fished, not hidden away in the basement like a demented in-law." We both have experience with this species. I watch as Dirt easily drops the ungainly fly forty feet away and about ten feet up from the tail of a long, deep run, just ahead of a large trout. While doing so, he makes a slight reach upstream that imparts a slight mend in the line in just the right place to cheat drag from the current, all this while the cast is whistling through the air for brief seconds. Beautiful. Playing with cane is sensual. The feel is soft, gentle and responsive. Like a good woman Dirt says. Graphite rods are tools and work well, but cane moves fly fishing to another realm. Someday I'd buy a couple – a nice four like Dirt's and a wind cheating seven-weight. And Dirt is one of the finest casters I've ever scene – in Montana, in Iceland, Tasmania - anywhere. He once held several line-class world records for steelhead caught while working the enormous coastal rivers of British Columbia back in the long-ago years when he lived on the west coast. I've seen photos of him holding enormous fish while leaning against a large downed Douglas Fir. He's standing there in a starkly honest black-and-white photograph with long, dark hair and a face that hasn't seen a razor for several days looking like he is truly living according to one of our more cherished dictums "Think like outlaw," or in other words "Keep a low profile and try and stay below the radar." We've both found that life is a little bit less difficult if we practice those three words. We both like people and enjoy being around them, but we are also loners at heart preferring our own company for days on end at times. Then we become lonely for the madness of our species and jump back into the fray. Parts of Montana are still open enough and honest enough to let those of us who need and thrive under such a routine have our curious ways.

A brown attacks the hopper within three feet of drift. Dirt sets the hook, plays the fish as it sounds to hold along the bronze-colored cobble. The fish rattles its head in anger and then reaches for the sky in a series of silver-spray leaps. Each time the brown goes to the air, Dirt maintains a firm connection with the fish and backs downstream a step or two. By the time the three-pound trout comes to his feet, both angler and fish are well below the run and the other browns are still feeding. Dirt is modest about all aspects of his life but one. His fishing ability. Put aside the fact that he is a fine artist on canvas, on the water he is a master. As he told me once after a few belts of scotch, "I can take trout where others can't even see a damn fish. That comes from many years of working water, staring at water and being fortunate to fish with the really good ones – Charles Brooks, LaFontaine and some of the old-timers around here who've sadly all died off. And I was fortunate to get to know Roderick Haig-Brown a little bit a year or so before he died. He guided me in the direction of the lyricism and rhythm of rivers and nature. I value the time I've spent with those men as much as anything in this life." From what I'd observed a number of times, he wasn't boasting. Dirt has a form of radar that separates fly fishermen into at least two groups - those that are so good it's spooky and those who are merely skillful. Some days I've watched him work a woolly bugger well below the surface, watched him bounce the weighted thing along the bottom and then swiftly raise his rod. Then I'd stare in amazement as a twenty-inch brown would come flying through the water and way up above the river shaking its colorful body in stunned rage at the audacity that any human could have found it hiding beneath a tangle of submerged roots in the dark waters. Dirt plays the fish fairly and quickly, admires the almost spectral gold, bronze, copper, black, white and red that large, wild browns carry with them through life, and then he turns the fish loose, smiling and laughing - a strong, yet muted sound. He'll turn to me, eyes glowing, and say "That's what it's all about Ed, my man," and he'll move a bit upriver and take another fish. How, I'll never know. I can't see him doing anything different from me and I never see what triggers his strike - no subtle shift in line movement, no shadowy flash from below. Nothing. His intuition, no his artistry, is a mystery to me. A joyful fascination. He takes three more trout of the same size or larger from the run, then walks over and sits beside me on a dead cottonwood that rests along the smooth, rock bank like a large, stately, gray scarecrow. Or something like that. Maybe Dirt will paint the scene in his own way someday.

"Give me one of those dried-out humps of yours," and I shake a Camel up from my pack, bits of tobacco flying off on the wind. He pulls an old lighter from a shirt pocket and lights the thing, inhales deeply, coughs a little and says "You're the only bastard I know who likes these the way I do. Stale and harsh. Here take a hit of this," and a silver flask appears out of nowhere. It is etched with the likeness of a sea-run brown he'd caught down in Tierra del Fuego after casting endlessly for eternal days in the constant, raging wind. The trout weighed over thirty pounds. He told me the fish ran him two miles down river towards the sea before finally tiring. When Dirt reached down to tail the fish, the tippet snapped, but the brown was exhausted to the point where it merely rolled over on its side, gills pulsing trying to suck down oxygen in the shallow water. That was years ago in his renegade angler days. Days when he skulked around like his browns, fishing all over the West and the world with an assortment of crazed friends - Iceland, Morocco, Mongolia, Fiji, the hidden mountain rivers along the Yukon-Northwest

Territories border around the Arctic Circle and the vast barren ground flows of that territory back when few outsiders knew of their existence, let alone fished them. When it came to fly fishing, he'd seen and done most all of it. He's had it too with the invasion by image-conscious morons who throw money at the local guides like they are indentured servants. Dirt prefers to work subtle, sophisticated water that requires stealth, patient and vision, the stuff that fails to catch the superficial interest of the new-comer pretenders. Small rivers that look like a little bit of nothing to the inexperienced. That's one of the reasons I like the guy. No bullshit. I drink some of his ever-present single-malt scotch in the ninety-degree summer heat. Quite thirst quenching. Yes indeed it is. I hand the flask. He takes a drink and puts it away somewhere. We smoke without talking, observing several browns feeding along a crease in the river above us. The big trout are keyed to the sound of the grasshoppers "splatting" on the water's surface, homing in like wolves and crunching down on the insects. Then they return to their holding spots. Efficient. Businesslike. Predacious. I love brown trout.

"Qualls tells me you're skulking about some trying to help out Liz Jones. Any luck? Or are you hypnotized by her looks and mooning around once more," and the laugh appears again out of thin air. " She's a quality lady and makes my head turn and eyes brighten just from the sound of her laugh. Damn! I should write a book."

"You're a painter."

"Since when do you have to be qualified to write? They pay you."

"Good point," and I touch off another cigarette. "I went over and talked with Qualls this morning. By the way, did you know he just spent two weeks in LA studying that place's DARE program? Said LA makes Biederbeck look like peace on earth. He rode with vice cops at night. Drive-by shootings. Gang fights. Bodies sprawled on sidewalks. In the middle of streets. Blood, drugs, gunfire everywhere. Called it hell on earth."

"Yeah. He mentioned it the other night. Said he picked up a lot of information on how to spot the gang bangers that have moved out this way to escape the heat in California. The thugs set up little kingdoms of their own out here," I say. "He and his officers have their hands full with all the crack and meth being dealt here. Time to institute a little Old West justice, I think."

Perhaps," said Dirt. The flask has appeared out of nowhere again. He takes another pull on the whiskey and then hands it to me. "Qualls said that he thinks Sam killed Mark. No matter how he tries, he can't see it any other way. He believes they'd been drinking a lot, had an argument and one thing led to another. Happens all the time or often enough. He can't find anyone who knows anything or has seen anything to alter that scenario. And some people around town said the two had been cool towards each other for days before the murder. The thing that bothers him is that a very valuable sapphire ring Grace always wore is missing. No one can find it and Sam just stares off into space whenever anybody asks him about it. But hell, from what I've heard from Liz, that's all he's capable of, at least for now. Who knows? Maybe he killed Grace for the ring and then lost it in the dirt out there. Anything is possible, but the ring bothers me. Bothers me a lot, but as Qualls said 'One thing led to another.'"

Dirt sputters over a sip of scotch from his mysterious flask. "One thing led to another. Lord spare me from fools. Someone blows Sam's head off and then cuts him to pieces. No drunk I know would do that, and I've met a few. One thing led to another, my ass. I've fished and bird hunted with Sam. Gotten drunk with him once or twice..."

"Once or twice?"

"If I may be allowed to finish. Hell, Sam played it straight and he was low-key all the time. Sure, he and Grace argued. They'd been friends since they were kids and those arguments were nothing more than some whiskey talking its head off, a little steam being blown off. We all know Grace was a bit on the grandiose side of life when he had a snoot full. Some of us get that way," says Dirt and he looks at me with a wise-ass grin.

"Glad to say that you recognize that personal short coming, Dirt. You really are becoming a much better person. We're all please with your progress."

"Yeah, and the horse you rode in on sport," says Dirt. Sometimes it was tough leaning against the same bar when Mark had a load on. What friends are worth hanging out with when they're three sheets to the wind, damnit? The two of them have been close to blows arguing over whether a .270 or a 30.06 is the best gun for mule deer. Same thing with radial tires. Toyos or Coopers. They almost got into a fistfight one night disagreeing about whether natural or artificial dubbing works best on Hare's ear nymphs. As for the Cubs or Giants, that's dangerous country, Ed. Even when he had a buzz going, though, Sam kept things pretty much together. Violence wasn't his style. If anything, Sam would pull into himself or play the peace maker. One or the other. Never the instigator. Arguing about nothing or damn everything is just the way it's always been with those two. No big deal. Sam didn't do it. I'll stake my reputation on it."

"That should make him feel better."

"God, I bless the day I met you, Bouchee. You define the term 'friendship,' and Dirt passes me the flask and says "Kill it. There's more around here some place. And I'm with you on the ring. Sam is no thief. He's never stiffed anyone that I know of. Somehow he always pays his bills. Maybe he does come from big money and that money comes to the rescue when Sam is hard up against it. You tell me. Grace loves that ring and is always flashing that damn thing around town. could see the size of that stone. I kept telling him to put it in a safe deposit box before someone tore his arm off him for it. We get some nasty people drifting through here. A ring like that, even pawned, will buy a lot of dope and booze, and a room to do it all in for months. There's rough trade that thinks nothing of killing for twenty bucks, hell just for the killing. That ring always looked like big trouble waiting to happen to me. And it's beginning to look like he should've taken my advice" and he laughs to himself, eyes going distant for awhile. "I liked Mark, always have. Same way with Sam. Come on here. Tell me what you think. What's the feeling in your gut? You've got fair instincts except when it comes to trout, buying used shotguns and pickups."

He reaches for the flask. The thing not only seems to

appear and disappear as if by magic, it is also bottomless. The scotch is starting to taste pretty good now. I take another drink and feel it slide warmly down into my stomach.

"Qualls usually gets it on the nose, but something doesn't feel right about this. I know Sam some. Shot Huns with him last fall on the bench country below the Buffalos for a week straight. You know, when we had those not too cool, overcast days and the birds were all over the place?..."

"He shot the Huns. You made a lot of noise from what I heard. Filled the sky with lead as they say in the hook-and-bullet rags. Give up that damn Beretta and buy that sixteen Darne of mine. You'll knock down birds with that gun. Take my word on this Ed. Bird hunting is a hell of a lot more fun when you hit something once in awhile."

"Our friendship is special, Dirt, sort of like what I have going with my ex-wife." I take some more of his whiskey.

"Don't get me started on that. Anything else on Sam?"

"Only that his psychiatric evaluation came out suggesting that he was anything but fit to stand trial. Completely out of touch and disorientated or something like that. When I called his doctor, he told me that psychotic comes close and that 'he's completely gone.' Those were his words. 'Completely gone.' And the autopsy report on Mark doesn't help much. A shotgun did the killing and either a ragged-edged knife or something as heavy as a chainsaw did the rest. What's to find out, especially after being in the ground for so long? I'm going up to the logging site tomorrow morning and check things out. Maybe I'll pick up on something the cops missed. I doubt it. I'll probably tell Liz to save her money. I'd like to help, but I don't think so on this one. The whole situation, what little I know about it, feels strange. I'll let you know what I find when I get back in the evening. You going to be in?"

"Have to be. Thursday bartender got busted for a DUI. Trying to make a call on his cell phone and steer with his knees. Nailed the side of Slump Borrow's fly shop, though that rickety old place needed leveling to begin with. Quite a sight seeing the truck three-quarters of the way in the building, ass-end sticking out with those red-and-white "Free Tibet" bumper stickers. Wrecked that great old '52 Dodge truck of his in the process. Now that's the true, damn shame of the incident. Fool refused a breath test and now he can't drive for ninety days." Dirt gets up groaning some with the stiff joints and aches of late middle-age. "There's something wrong with this Ed. I know you trust Qualls' judgment, but he's not on the right track with this. Even a good cop misses one every now and then. There's darkness here. Coal black darkness. I feel it. Watch yourself and take along that silly dog of yours when you go up to Indian Creek. His instincts are a lot better than yours. He'll tell you if you need to get away from the place in a hurry as in real damn fast. Then again, he's been around you so long he's probably close to brain-dead."

Dirt winks, smiles and laughs his laugh, but I can see he is serious and is truly bothered by the entire swirling mess that is Mark Grace's murder.

We fish some more, until dark, and catch plenty more browns. Big, bright ones. A nice afternoon. It would turn out to be one of the last for awhile.

~ ~ ~

The Dog and I lurch and bounce around in the cab of the truck as we roll to the murder site alongside Indian Creek. Mozart's Vesperae de Dominca is rocking away on the CD. I would have preferred Just Another Band From East L.A. by Los Lobos, but The Dog is adamant about Mozart and puts his paw down. He stared sullenly out the window, dead silent, until I made the switch. When they get this way there's nothing you can do. I've learned, painfully, over the years that the art of small compromise saves many a relationship. This is true in spades where this animal is concerned. Within a few miles of cruising north on the highway paralleling The Hart he is his old self again. The Dog I know and love is now barking at deer standing on the side of the road as we whiz by and giving me that big-eyed look that melts my heart. I know, this probably seems twisted, but you make the most of what they give you. Indian Creek flows clear and blue as we follow it along the gravel road. There are few ranches or cabins this far up. The only person I spot was a bearded man standing in the middle of the stream in hip waders. He's holding an old Fenwick glass fly rod. The off-red color of that well-made relic is unmistakable. The guy's probably fishing for Yellowstone cutts that like this cold, clean water way up here. Who knows? He looks away as we lurch past. People out here aren't unfriendly. They just like their privacy, and some of them are full-time recluses. I understand the concept. I get this way some times, usually when I'm behind on the bills, working on a book or merely in the need for some time alone. We bounce and lurch on until we reach the murder site thirty minutes later.

Looking through the cracked and chipped windshield – I think that even new cars come with these in this state - I can see that perhaps twenty acres is logged. Stumps and blackened piles of partially burned slash are piled throughout the scarred earth that is deeply marked by the treads of the skid cat, the logging truck that hauls the limbed timber to the mill and by what looks like pickup trucks. Probably those of Jones and Grace. The skid cat Liz has described is still wedged up against the large Ponderosa. Even from here I can see the torn hoses, scratch marks in the faded, dirty yellow paint, and a grimy streak of diesel fuel that runs down one side of the engine and over the rusting black frame. The rig's trashed. Repairing the machine will probably cost more than it was worth. A large pile of trimmed logs is stacked off to the right. The air smells thickly of pine sap and resin. Oil cans, wine bottles, beer cans, whiskey bottles and other garbage litters the ground around the area where the cops discovered the buried body parts. This is next to a group of old Ponderosa pines that are still standing near the stream. These stately trees survived because all sales are now required by the Forest Service to leave a minimum buffer zone of at least one-hundred feet between flowing water and where the cutting occurs. The recent regs resulted from a series of lawsuits and appeals by various environmental groups around the West. That was a major accomplishment on their part. This new rule helps check the flow of sediment that rain and snowmelt in the spring wash into the water, sediments that choke both fish and aquatic insect life, and bury streambed gravels trout use for spawning.

The Dog leaps out the open window on his side of the truck as soon as we stop, landing in a heap with a grunt, rights himself, and bounds off, nose to the ground, straight for the now-open grave. Yellow police tape is posted in a large rectangle around the area and also where the two men had pitched their camp. Aside from removing the body remains, camping gear, food, tools and a few other objects for fingerprints, nothing has really changed since the crime was committed sometime in June. I walk to the creek to look for feeding fish. First things first. Completely hopeless in this regard. I became hooked on this passionate pursuit as a little kid when I used to walk alongside small streams referred to as "kids' creeks" out this way. I'd drop a worm in every small pocket and glide, catching small trout after small trout. The wonder and magic of those childhood days has stayed with me, grown even stronger, all these years. The band of trees along the riparian zone helps some with the dirt and mud, but even with the scarce rainfall this summer, long, greasy-looking ribbons of silt stretch over what once was a clear, free-flowing streamed of multi-colored rocks. A large pool is now filled in with the crud and the water is pushed over to the far bank, eating away at the rocky soil. Several trees are already lying across the creek, having lost their hold on things with the erosion. I don't see any fish and only a few small caddis flies are whirring among the bank side bushes. This quarter-mile part of Indian Creek is ruined for at least a few years. I turn and walk to where they'd found Mark's remains.

As I look ahead I see raw ground that slopes gradually up to thickly-timbered hills that give way to another ridge covered in pine. Beyond this the peaks of the Nortons are barren of snow, rising in soft shades of purple and gray into a sun-baked, white-blue sky. The scars from the logging, along with the damaged stream, juxtaposed with the rich growth of pines and the untamed peaks make for a disturbing vision. I know we need lumber, but at what cost? Give me plastic. The choice, quality stuff oh so good and true. Ruining this place seems a high price to pay for new homes with wrap-around decks and wood-shaked roofs. The frustration that comes with the realization that there is no quick-fix solution to this problem makes me groan out loud and say "Screw it all." An incurable optimist at heart. My words bring The Dog running up to me in a grouse-scent-inspired zigzag. Halfway to me he hangs an abrupt left and disappears into a mat of thick brush. He vanishes. I can hear him pushing through the tangles and snorting with excitement. Moments later five spruce grouse burst straight up in a whir of beating wings and crazed cackles. Seeing me, they veer sharply and cut straight across the creek. They are soon out of sight over a slight rise a hundred yards away. I approach the place where I last saw my Springer. There is no sound coming from within. A sure sign that he's found something. The Dog turns intensely silent whenever he is on the track or turns up something he thinks is of value. Perhaps another grouse or two. More likely a Columbian ground squirrel. A few steps more and one more grouse explodes from the cover followed by The Dog who almost makes it free of the bushes, head, neck and front paws extending, reaching for the frantic grouse, but he falls back to earth just missing his quarry. I hear a groan from the brush. The last I see of the dark-feathered bird is a blur of earth-tone feathers racing low to the ground. Seconds later my buddy is panting at my feet, giving me a look that says "Where's your gun?" and another one that probably adds "What difference would it make? You hardly ever hit anything, anyway?" My shooting prowess is legendary. I used to be a fair wing shot back in the days when I drank way too much. Now that I don't, my accuracy has fallen, dramatically. None of us can figure this unimportant conundrum out. There are, no doubt, plenty of birds wandering through the cover here. A nice place to hunt if you like to work murder sites and prefer your upland shooting on the weird side. I'd take a pass on this one.

"In a few weeks we'll do it for real, buddy. Just hang on. Remember, you're the patient one here," and he waved his bobbed tail and raced away, nose down like always, happy as hell while my mind drifted off on a riff about patience, about how I ran out of gas when good things with an extraordinary woman were in sight. If I could have lasted a few more weeks, given the lady a little more time to make her decision in her own way, but I couldn't, losing my cool from anxiety and confusion, then blowing the whole thing away with a drunken phone call five or six or seven years ago. That stretch still seems unreal. Like it never happened. The pain I feel whenever I think about her tells me differently. If I'd only held on, pushed through the tough minutes that pass like hideous years, life would have been much better. Fuller. Wilder. Instead, I fell apart and lost it. Biggest mistake of my life and I've made a few. Haven't heard from her since that horrible night. I will always miss and love her, though. She was a true, good experience in my life. Screwed up again. I hate when this stuff wanders through my mind, but I can't do anything to stop it. Maybe I should take up Yoga or meditation. I caught myself before things turned big-league morose. Shook my head. Lit a smoke and moved to the grave, ducking under the yellow tape that was already bleaching towards a puke-white in the sun.

It is a strange feeling moving through a place where someone you know has been killed and literally cut to pieces. The hole where Grace was dumped measures about four by six feet and maybe three deep. It appears to have been dug in haste. Spadefuls of dirt and stone are scattered about in all directions. The hole itself is more circular rather than rectangular in shape. Along the edges, neat mounds of earth are piled, the work of the cops when they unearthed the remains a few weeks ago. I look down and even with the distance of time and weather, can still see that the dirt is stained dark red-brown from Mark's blood. Around the grave splotches of the stuff are visible. A shiver works its way up my back and down my arms. My forehead tingles. I don't like being here at all. How anyone can make a living as a coroner or a cop, I have no idea. There is nothing else to see. Nothing except booze bottles and a crushed can of maple syrup from Vermont. At least they had good taste when it came to breakfast. A trail of dried blood, a lot of it still visible, not completely washed into the ground yet, connects with the campsite. Very little rain this summer and fire season that promises to be brutal. I follow this for thirty feet and come to their fire ring. Chopped up logs, broken sticks, used wooden matches and more bottles are lying all over the place. Two stumps used as stools are facing each other across the fire pit. On one side the ground is scraped and disturbed. Disturbed - a good word to my way of thinking. Blood is thick here, dried and cracked like spilled enamel paint. I drop to my knees to get a closer look, afraid I'll find some hunks of Mark's flesh. I'm not disappointed. About six feet from the fire I spot an inch-long, narrow strip of skin with light hair on it. Probably from an arm or leg. I doubt the investigators missed this. There'd probably been so much of Grace lying around here, they'd gotten all they needed for forensic purposes. I stand up feeling slightly queasy. Some people actually enjoy gutting the big game they shoot. I'm one of them. Seeing human blood and flesh goes beyond the pale for me. I light a cigarette, suck the smoke way down and inhale again before I've completely exhaled the first puff. I start to feel better or at least, not quite as bad.

I can see distinct footprints made by work boots in two sizes. Grace being a bigger man than Sam, most likely made the larger ones. The police have been circumspect here. I only notice two other pairs of tracks and they've kept to a narrow line either right behind each other or side-by-side. As I begin to back away, I notice large, deeper footprints about ten feet from the killing spot. Just two of them. Large. Size 13 or 14. I look for quite some time and am unable to find any others. Unfortunately, some of the ground in the area looks like it's been swept over with a broom, or more likely, a pine bough. Probably nothing, but I feel a twinge in my stomach and a swift jolt of paranoia or fear fires through my head. My instincts, what is left of them, are rarely off the mark. Whenever I ignore them, something strange, bad or painful happens. I decide to call The Dog and leave.

He is rooting around in some dense grass fifty yards away. As soon as I look at him, he starts running towards me. His radar is much better then mine. He covers the distance in seconds. I notice something, long, dark and hairy in his mouth. My mind conjures up all sorts of disgusting objects as it is prone to do – a dead mouse, bear scat, even a piece of Mark Grace. The Imp of the Perverse as Poe called. The Dog drops the object at my feet. Thick, gnarled, brown almost black hair. It is the end of a tail from a large animal approximately the diameter of a twelve-gauge shotgun shell. It's not from a deer or an elk or even a cow. The hair would be thinner and have some tan and white mixed in. Probably a moose. There are some holding in the marshy areas along streams higher up in these green hills. The animal was probably shot last year, but the tail is in pretty good shape. Dirt will know. He's a repository for all sorts of esoteric, borderline useless information. Like the fact that the capital of Nevada, Carson City, is farther west than LA or that Andre Dawson is the only player to win the National League MVP while playing for a last-place team in 1987. The Cubs, of course. But Andre did blast forty-nine homers that season. And without the aid of injecting various steroids unlike Barry Bonds, Sammy Sosa, Mark McGuire and so many other power hitters from the mid-nineties on through 2004. Nothing is sacred or as it used to be and for a sentimental traditionalist such as myself, doped up home run records and ridiculous salaries have all the romance and charm of B-1 bomber or the thankfully retired *Friends* TV series. I mean, that was really sophomoric junk, but as usual, I digress.

We climb in my side of the truck and head back to Biederbeck with a planned stop along a nice run of water in The Hart. The hoppers are flying and clacking through the hot air now. I can never catch too many big browns. I figure that there's always a chance that the boys running the show in D.C. could have a few too many at some horrible inner-Beltway bar, lose their grip on what passes for civility in that town big time and take us all along for the last ride. Take the fishing when you can. I put on Los Lobos - "Angels With Dirty Faces." Whatever. The Dog pretends that he likes the music, but soon has his head thrust far out the window, large ears riding the rushing air like horizontal sails. He's happy.

~ ~ ~

Happy Hour at Ray's Bleachers is always something of an event even though it is fairly predictable in its slightly bizarre ebb and flow as practiced by the regulars. Writers, painters, photographers, fishing guides, guys from the train yards, and Lord only knows who else wanders in. Biederbeck attracts the hard-core of the so-called artistic world along with the rough and tumble from the cattle, logging and other more traditional Montana professions like armed robbery and vagrancy. Most of them do what they do for the sake of doing it. Money, fame, respect are foreign concepts to many of them. As a friend said to me when I first moved here, "Don't worry about screwing up. Anything you can ever think of doing, has already been done here. More than once." This both set me at ease and presented something of a challenge. Early on I took perverse pride in making outrageous errors in judgment, things others would never think of trying. Executing these bits of madness with a certain flair and panache was my art. I'm sure they still loved me in Whitefish. A friend from there called awhile ago and told me that the pin setters at the bowling alley are working once again. For the most part I've left this juvenile silliness to the younger sports lounging around town, though I have a few schemes working in the back of my head, but the time isn't right and as some of us know, timing is everything. Two friends of mine, artists, are hunkered down over scotch and Marlboros discussing the proper proportions for painting the adiposal fin of golden trout. A hot topic, I'm sure. They are way into it, hands gesturing, clouds of smoke rising, voice levels climbing. I look straight ahead, deftly avoiding eye contact, and walk on by. Another couple of acquaintances, a landscape photographer and a well-known adventure travel writer, are leaning against the bar drinking what looks like tequila from highball glasses. As I stroll swiftly past them I hear the words "dynamite," "plastique," "game warden" and "dip net." I thought they were over that delicate form of angling, but I guess when you find something that works you stick with it until it breaks or Fish, Wildlife and Parks busts you. Only six p.m. Early yet and the place is pretty slow by Ray's standards. Another thirty minutes and the atmosphere will be a notch or two higher. I spot Dirt at the far end of the long mahogany bar polishing wine glasses and staring through the open blinds at a passing train. I can hear and feel the rumble of the six helper engines as they begin to power up their thousands of horsepower for the climb over the pass fifteen miles to the west. By the time I reach the stool in front of him a triple of Beam on the rocks is waiting. I thought I'd been keeping an eye on the guy, but he got this drink past me, just like the flask, without any discernible motion. He finishes shining a last crystal glass, sets it down and says "You know, I've been watching these damn trains for years and I still haven't figured out what they're hauling around in those big, solid, silver tankers, the ones with the bulging sides that look like they're ready to explode. You have to wonder what's rolling around inside those things. You'd think the crack reporter at the paper might take at least a small interest in whatever it is the railroad is hauling through town. Hell no. Much more interested in another bear mauling in the Park. Who cares? Those tankers are probably full of toxic or radioactive waste that they're dumping outside of town, upriver. Cyanide. Mercury from a pulp mill. You name it. That would certainly go a long way towards explaining some of the things I see going on in here," and he looks down at the four patrons I just passed and shakes his head, then looks at me and winks. "Bouchee, I know why you like it here so much. You can conjure up in that sick head of yours the weirdest shit imaginable and put most of it into practice. Back in Whitefish they were so damn tight-assed they always wanted to put you away. In this place, nobody notices or if they do, they don't give a damn or better still, most of the nut cases in this place dig your act."

"Don't sell me short Dirt. I've got a little thing goin' here, but it's a few months off," and I finish the whiskey, shove the glass across the bar and light a smoke before he can say a thing.

"Don't doubt that for a minute. Just give me a clue when to leave town if it involves serious mayhem, Bouchee. Please?"

"I'm beyond that sort of childish behavior. What I have in mind, and the key word is 'mind', is far more expansive, more elegant. You might even say ornate. You'll love it. Trust me."

"You're completely nuts, Eddie my man, but I love you in that special way," and another triple Beam is waiting right there before me. I never saw it coming. I look up at Dirt. He winks and laughs. "We're both lunatics, so is everyone in this town. Completely gone. The way it should be."

"May it always be so."

"Don't start with that crap again," and Dirt works on a glass of scotch. And yes, I don't have any idea how it appeared either. "Find anything at Indian Creek? Wait a minute. I'll be right back." He moves down to pour another round for the eight or nine people now gathered at the other end of the bar. The talk has attained a volume where snatches of conversation reach me. How in the hell they manage to fuse adiposal fins with dynamite, I'll never know, but everyone down that way is contributing to the conversation, heads nodding up and down, drink glasses slamming the bar to make a point. I love this place. Like Dirt said, we're all completely nuts.

Happy Hour. In most places that means two drinks for the price of one. Here I can well imagine that the prices doubled, maybe tripled. It doesn't matter. Any excuse will do and the only money Dirt lets me spend is on tips. He is good to those who work for him or "with him" as he likes to say. Why this is so, why the generosity is directed at me, I don't know. It is the way it is. I've at least learned not to question or examine uncommon good fortune. Good food and strong drinks at no cost - a fine deal. Another of the town's many artists staggers in, soaking wet and wearing only a pair of jeans. He is yelling that a "monster trout" had taken his fly, charged down river and eventually pulled him into the water. No one pays much attention. This has happened before. Often. By the time he slogs his way to the bar, a drink is waiting for him. Old Overholt on the rocks with a cherry and a dash of orange bitters. A man of taste and discrimination. I'd empty mine, but Dirt had a another waiting by the time I turn back from Biederbeck's version of the Algonquin Round Table. I'd given up long ago trying to figure out how he does this stuff. It is well beyond my abilities of understanding.

"So, what'd you find?"

"Mostly what the cops left, along with a lot of dried blood, a piece of flesh and a trashed trout stream. Not a pleasant place to spend an afternoon. Gave me the creeps." I reach into my hip pocket looking for more matches and happen upon the end of the tail The Dog found. "And this. What the hell kind of animal does it belong to? Moose?"

Dirt takes the furry thing from me. It is about the size of a Hoyo de Monterrey Rothschild cigar, maduro wrapper. He holds it up to the early evening light slanting in through the window. He twists and turns around in front of eyes. Slides his thumb and forefinger back and forth along the hair. Even sniffs it. Then he smiles and his gray mustache rose with the grin.

"Not moose. Looks like the end of a buffalo tail. Thick

enough. Siksikas used the whole thing as a quirt. Tails are stout enough to bang the hell out of someone. Used to knock the Crow and Northern Cheyenne senseless in many of their horseback battles back when Montana was Montana."

"You can tell all that by smelling the thing?"

"Hell no. That was for show. I've read a lot on the Siksikas and I can tell by the coarseness and color of the hair. I helped skin a few of the buffalo they shot wandering out of the Park last winter. Everyone freaking out about shooting the things. They never wintered up there historically. Try spending a winter on that plateau at 8,000 feet. Fifty below zero. Wind howling all the time. Blizzards. Awful cold. Reminds me of my third, or was it fifth, wife. Fine woman. The finest. Where do the PETA morons think that the poor animals are going to head? Down in the valley where it's not as cold, of course. Animal rights jerks can't think beyond their noses. Pinheads. There's way too many buffalo for the land to carry, not to mention the elk. Chewing the Yellowstone down to dirt. Never did care much for National Parks in the first place. Nothing but glorified zoos." He turns from me and spends a few minutes muttering and checking the moisture level of his cigar humidor. "As for this, the tails on the buffalo we butchered were just like this one. Longer, but this one looks like it's been clipped well above the base. Moose is close, but its hair is darker and it is not quite as thick. Where'd your dog find it?"

"Not far from the grave and murder site, in the middle of some thick grass about fifty yards away and not too far from the creek. He turns up all sorts of crazy stuff with that nose of his. Fish bones, deer carcasses, old discarded hamburger wrappers, cigar butts. You've seen him work."

Dirt finishes his scotch and sets the glass down. Mine is full again and I'm starting to feel pretty good from all the whiskey. "Yes I have. A curious thing to see. Damn good dog and he works close, especially when there's garbage afoot. Never gets out of range. Dog like that doesn't come along every day. He's something special. Sure as hell is."

Dirt actually means what he just said. He and The Dog have a close friendship that involved lots of yips, howls and slobbering kisses exchanged by each of them. Every time the two run into each other, on Main, in Ray's, at church – yes they both go to church on Sunday's at St. Mary's right next to the fly fishing museum - Dirt drops to his knees, gently grabs The Dog's floppy ears and gives The Dog a big kiss. The animal howls with pleasure. Dirt claims an Irish Setter he had a long time ago showed him this form of canine pleasure after a long day hunting ringnecks outside of Mobridge, North Dakota. I can't watch anymore and neither can anyone else in town, but the two of them are fast friends and this was their own personal ritual.

"All I can say to you, Eddie, is that if you track down where this tail comes from and who left it behind up there, you'll have Mark's killer and a lot more. Something most unusual and mean is involved in this, maybe worse than murder. Sick. I mean it when I say this is dark. There's trouble running all through this thing and all around Liz, Sam," and Dirt leans down right in front of my face" and you.

Holding his gaze, I drain my drink, say "See you later" and head for the exit.

"Bouchee. You probably should pay more attention to that dog. He has a lot more sense than you do."

I turn around and nod in agreement. Then I walk out the door and back to the office. Just another delightful evening in Biederbeck.

~ ~ ~

The bearded man sees Bouchee driving along the road in his truck, hears the coughing roar belching out of the ratty muffler and takes in the thin cloud of bluish smoke that drifts on the air in its wake. He doesn't know who Bouchee is. He has no reason to. Right now he's occupied with looking for the best places to secure his nets in September, a time when the brown trout will be running upstream to their spawning grounds. He carries a fly rod with him to defuse any suspicions that might arise concerning someone wading the stream for no apparent purpose. In this state not many people spend time walking up the middle of a prime trout stream without carrying a fly rod. Some things just aren't done. To his way of thinking, fly fishing has no apparent purpose, but playing the game, paying attention to details is what has kept him free all these years. Three small feeder creeks come into the main flow just above where he's standing right now. Two spring creeks pouring cold, clear water run in from his left and another sparkling free-stone style down from the Norton's joins on the right. As he has in past years, he decides to string the gill net across Indian Creek just below the three. Browns like to dig their redds in small- to medium-size gravels in clean water full of oxygen. Ideal conditions for the hundreds of thousands of fertilized eggs to incubate and hatch later on. If one-in-a-thousand, perhaps as few as one-in-ten-thousand reaches a foot or more in length, brown trout in this small drainage will survive. The majority of males and females of this species hold down in the main river following spawning. They stay there through July before making the sixty- to seventy-mile journey into The Hart, swimming up along the many twisting, gravelly, deep pools and slick runs of its lengths. Then the fish turn right, into Indian Creek and push against the swift current another twenty miles to these and other small creeks. All of this takes place from August through early November, give or take a week or two. The length of the days, angle of sunlight and cooling water temperatures all combine to trigger this breeding reflex when conditions are optimal. Some of the fish spawn in Indian Creek and even slower and warmer The Hart. It all depends on where the fish had hatched in the first place. Each individual is imprinted with the distinct chemical qualities of its natal waters and homes in on its birth place with unerring accuracy year after year century after century. Maybe they are assisted in this riverine navigation by a magnetic pulling from the planets and stars. Maybe they can taste the difference in the water or perhaps the trout detect a subtle shift in the ionization of the water of a certain stream. Maybe they are in love. Who really knows? For that matter, what difference does it make? All he cares about is locating the prime spot to net hundreds of these large fish along with a fair amount of Yellowstone cutthroat trout that stay in Indian creek all year. And no one lives this far up except for him. The only people he ever sees are hunters headed for country higher up and the stray fly fishermen searching for new water. Funny how so many of them have flat tires on this stretch. Sharp rocks or something. His meat distributor, the one back in Omaha who deals with the poached buffalo, has a willing market for these wild fish from Montana. He can handle all the trout the bearded man is able to deliver, and at four bucks per pound gutted with the heads left on. The fancy restaurants in the big cities like to serve them this way, and "So much the better," he thinks. More cash for me. Some even want the fish whole, guts and all. Better still. More weight. Less work. More money. This man thinks about this often. When he does so he runs his fingers through his dark hair and through his long beard, unconsciously tying and untying overhand knots in the bushy hair with deft movements of his fingers. He's eaten the browns before. Fried them. Baked them. Sautéed them. Poached them in white wine. No matter how he prepares them, he thinks they taste gamy, a little rotten. The cutthroat are a little better, but he can't imagine why anyone will spend good money to eat the things in a fancy restaurant. He much prefers red meat – beef, elk, moose, bison. Bison most of all and he smiles at this. As for eating the trout, he just shakes his head and goes about his business.

So, he plans to string his net across the water right where he is standing, securing it to a weathered cottonwood on one bank and to a large quaking aspen on the other. Last year the net held so many fish one time that their weight bent, then broke the tree it was tied to. He makes sure that the tree he selects this time from the copse is stronger. He doesn't like to make mistakes of any kind, even small ones. He sees them as signs of weakness, wastes of time, indications of sloppy minds. He has contempt for those who are not thorough, strong, meticulous, tough. The trout will be stacked up here, staging for their move into the small creeks to spawn. He and Grace will work upstream for a half mile driving the browns and cutthroat into the net and to their deaths. The two of them will work from either side of Indian creek, stomping along, thrashing the water as they go with their feet and with large sticks. Some of the fish will escape between them, but most of the browns will swim pell-mell into the net, their gills catching on the thin weave of the device.

Two, or in a good year, three times he or Grace make the thousand-mile drive to Omaha in an old Sealtest Ice Cream truck that he picked up for a song up near Plentywood in the northeastern corner of the state some years ago. A few hundred dollars for parts, a little welding and other repair work, a plain brown paint job and they were in business. The trout always arrive cold and fresh in Nebraska. They can make the trip both ways in less than two full days. The man in Omaha pays in cash and covers the road expenses. Easy money. Twenty, thirty, even forty grand for two weeks work, but the illegal netting has done a number on the trout population in this stream and they'll be lucky to see fifteen thousand dollars this year. He is already scouting another stream that drops down from an even more out-of-the-way range of mountains up north. Last autumn he saw hundreds of large browns, some close to ten pounds and even some brook trout of a pound or two. These are the best eating species of trout and he's going to charge six bucks a pound for them. The new location adds more driving time to Omaha, but money is money and he refuse to work for anyone but himself. The idea of taking orders from anyone or following another's time schedule is more than repugnant to him than any other aspect of living he can conceive or has ever experienced. The insane desire for self-defined freedom, autonomy has led to him committing violent felonies including murder. These acts bothered him only slightly in the beginning. Now whatever he does, he does to survive and continue his way of living. Whether this involves breaking the law or hurting others is never factored in. None of this matters to him. Only running free counts now.

He also has a hate for most people. He considers them weak, incapable of decision and related action. Individuals with no code of behavior or consistency of response to what life deals out day after day. He is extremely intelligent and capable of comparing a current situation with similar ones he's experienced in the past. He runs through a list of options, possible courses of action in seconds, decides on the best path and moves on swiftly and confidently from that point. The hate is an emotion he feels most of the time – pure, white-hot rage. The rest of the feelings - joy, sorrow, fear, all the others - serve no purpose for him other than as gauges of what is occurring around and within him. He rides this edge of hate, the energy taking him to places few others know exist. When people get in his way ugly things happen. Not because he enjoys cruelty or meanness, but because he's learned over time that harsh, brutal action produces immediate results in his world. He grows angry with even the light weight he feels from people's casual glances. He considers these glances and other casual actions as intrusions in his life. These are resented. Anything beyond this drives him mad. He's been this way for most his life.

When he was a child, his father beat him with a thick leather belt when he was drunk, which was every day. This started when he was three or four, back when he had another name, one he'd totally forgotten or pushed far back in his memory. Now he called himself only Miskis. The name sounds powerful, elusive when he says it aloud, his deep, whiskey-and-cigarette graveled voice gives those six letters a feeling and a sense of power and an ominous hint of what rests within his soul.

At fifteen, after trying to run away from home more times than he could remember, he'd had enough. Even at this age he was already over six-feet tall with dark, stormy good looks that had not gone unnoticed by his female classmates and by a number of women around the area. He was keenly aware of his attraction to women. He knew what worked - his looks, a brooding silence and brief snatches of somber talk about his hard life. Wives, unmarried, divorced or widowed women, he'd slept with a lot of them. They'd taught him well in the complicated art of satisfying them sexually, which he discovered was as much a psychological realm as physical. He would no more than glance at an attractive female in a bar (he easily passed for twenty-one and no one really cared anyway in this tough town) or passing on the street and he instantly knew what she wanted and needed. All he had to do was make eye contact, focus his will on a woman and she was his. It was one of his gifts and perhaps a curse, too he sometimes thought. All of this sleeping with these women eased some of his pain, but also jaded his view of people and turned him cynical, indirectly fueling his growing rage and disgust with his others. Finally he'd had enough and snapped or what is more likely, discovered his real self. A predator of the most basic, and by the slightest of extensions, powerful sort. He fed off other's energy – fear, joy, self-confidence, insecurity, all of it.

So the days of abuse ended. One late afternoon he hid behind some bushes next to the old barn where his father always parked his car when he returned from work at the steel mill a dozen miles away in Sterling, Illinois. No one cared what happened to Miskis as a kid. Not at school. Not around town. Not out in the country where he lived. His mother was long gone. Had been for years. She'd run away with an aluminum siding salesman following a weekend of heavy drinking and sex at a local motel called The End of the Rainbow. He'd laugh whenever the name flashed across his mind. When he thinks of her anymore, infrequently, only a dim, out-of-focus image arises. Nothing as bright and intense as the electric colors of the motel's neon signs and trimmings. All he feels for her is a distant sense of loss that is more vague shadow image than anything resembling pain, practically nothing. Only one more sadness and disappointment in his brief life. His father would come home after a few hours of knocking back Boilermakers at a bar outside the mill called The Iron Worker, a local watering hole for the hot, dirty, exhausted men. Then he'd stagger through the back door, grab

Miskis and beat the hell out him. This would go on far into the night, until the old man would pass out. Teachers and others noticed the bruises, the smashed in nose, but this was a tough town and was back when people stayed out of others' family business.

That day when he was fifteen, was the day when he gave in to the dark strength inside him. It was only another in a eternal string of painful, deadly segments. One after another. Hellish in their ugly monotony. As the sun began to drop towards the horizon sinking down towards large fields of sprouting feed corn, he crouched low behind the bushes like a ghost. He held a rusty scythe used to hack down thistle around the house. He clutched the thing in both hands. Soon his father drove up the dirt lane, rolled to a stop that included bumping into the corner of the barn. He pushed open the car door. Pulling himself up using purchase his hands gained from grabbing the frame above the door window, his father teetered out of the car and began to lurch towards the screen door of the dilapidated house. He tripped and stumbled over garbage and neglected tools on his way.

"You son-of-a-bitch," he yelled to the empty house. No lights were on and the back screen door swung slowly back and forth on its hinges, making an eerie, metallic noise before banging hollowly on the its rotting wood frame. Those were the only sounds. No birds chirping with the sunset. No easy wind drifting through fresh green leaves budding on the gnarled oak trees that surrounded the un-mowed yard. Nothing.

"Get your ass over here. Right now, damnit."

He passed by the young Miskis and as he did so, the

youth leaped up and through the bushes. He swung the scythe as hard as he could, cleaving his father's head with the stroke. The headless torso dropped to the ground and flopped around briefly, though it seemed like forever to Miskis. The head rolled end-over-end before coming to a stop resting on the stump of its neck facing him. In the shifting shadows of sunset he thought he could see his father's eyes bore right through his soul burning with coal black hate. He thought he could see his father's thick lips worked briefly, mouthing what Miskis imagined, no absolutely knew, were the words "Worthless piece of shit." Their brutal message seared permanently in his mind, marking him forever. The boy Miskis was frozen in terror. Blood - it seemed like there were gallons of the stuff welling up as if from some vast underground reserve, and then, that blood ever so slowly sinking back into the ground - was all over the place. Gouts of the it had washed over his face and clothes. Noticing this pushed him into motion. He stripped naked, washed himself with the icy spray from the garden hose. The cold of the water cleared his head. He ran inside, dressing quickly and taking the money his father kept in an old White Owl cigar box on the kitchen counter. More than nine hundred dollars. Miskis skirted his father's body, clutching the box next to his chest. The dead eyes in the severed head stared at him. He shuddered and kicked the thing into the bushes. In the fading light a quick flash caught his eye. On the right hand of his father's lifeless body the boy saw a ring on the middle finger. A small, light-blue stone mounted in a gold setting glistened for an instant then went dull as the sun dropped below the horizon. The boy looked up at the old house for one last time and felt nothing. He got into the car. Started it up, he drove fast in the dark without headlights on U.S. 30, crossing into Iowa at Clinton, then worked his way along the back roads until he reached Nebraska. He was under age, a murderer in his teens, now homeless. Instead of worry or fear, Miskis felt a sense of exhilaration and freedom he'd never known before. He was glad he'd killed the old man. He realized that if backed into a corner again, he'd do the same thing to anyone, man or woman. His freedom was paramount. His only valuable and constant possession. He wondered if his father's head was still alive, if its eyes still worked so it could watch as day turned to night and the stars came out. Miskis laughed and screamed for miles. He could do whatever he wanted now. No one owned him anymore. No one could beat him black-and-blue ever again.

He ditched the car, rolling it into an overgrown irrigation ditch on a dirt two-track that ran alongside a vast wheat field in South Dakota a few hours southeast of the Black Hills and not far from a small town called Colome. He picked up a ride that took him all the way to the outskirts of Rapid City. One more day of hitching found him in Miles City, Montana where he got a room in a boarding house, found work swamping out the Range Rider Bar and another doing whatever jobs no one else wanted to do at the stockyards on the edge of town. Even at this age he hated working for others, but he kept his cool and hung around town for seven years, laying low and keeping to himself. At thirteen he looked eighteen, already over six feet with a good beard. By twenty the hard drinking, bar fights, whoring and sleepless nights had turned him hard. He could have been fifty or a rough thirty. No one bothers anyone in eastern Montana as long as they leave well enough alone, even today. Forty years ago, this was even more true. And the authorities never even came close to looking for him in Montana. Actually, they didn't spend much time trying to solve his father's murder. The papers were full of it, as they usually are, for a few days, then the matter faded from public awareness. The cops looked around and did all the routine things like trying to find Miskis, half-heartedly ran down a few dead-end leads, but nothing turned up and after a few months, the murder, while still an open case, was essentially a dead issue. By twenty he had a few thousand saved up and the name Miskis was his. Like many people, he followed baseball. Eddie Thomas Miksis played first base for the Cubs in the fifties. Some big dumb guy, thought the new Thomas. I'll use his name. Yah. Eddie Thomas Miksis stinks. So does Eddie Miskis or Ed Miskis, but just down and dirty Miskis is okay. Shift the "k" and the "s" and the name hisses at you like a snake. I like that. And so the Montana incarnation of Miskis appeared in 1961 way out on the high plains. The year Roger Maris broke Babe Ruth's homerun record. One year before the Cuban Missile Crisis.

Since that time he'd stopped working for anyone. He'd moved on to rolling and, when he felt it was in his best self-protective interests, even killing drunks and drifters up on the Hi-Line not far from the Canadian border, an area where almost no one lived or traveled through. He'd come upon their smoky little fires and squalid camps. He'd always bring some whiskey which was a sure ticket to a seat next to the flames. He could hold his liquor and most of the transients couldn't. They were already wet-head alcoholics. When they became shit faced as he put it, he'd kill them. Not always for the money, they rarely had more than a few bucks in their bindle. He often murdered them for the quick rush of evil that shot into his ever-darkening soul. Nothing sexual here, just cold old, basic evil. He never looked at his actions as good, bad or evil. He acted on impulse, a calculating response that was honed to survivalist perfection over the lonely, hard years, but impulse all the same. He did this for a long time, moving on to robbing and killing the young hippies, boys and girls, who hitchhiked across the state through the late seventies. It was amazing the amount of cash they carried on them and the expensive rings and even gold Rolex watches they wore. Miskis had no special love or driving need to murder people. Killing them was no big deal. The psychic juice he felt as he connected with their terror and horror when they realized their grizzly fates was something he fed on, but he did not need this energy in anyway resembling a junkie. It was only something that he noticed, was aware of and noticed how it affected him. The killing and the getting away with it came naturally to him. Bringing death to others was a natural part of his life, one that was at once logical, orderly and necessary. He was merely keeping the promise he'd made to himself when he'd fled Illinois so long ago. He experienced anger and a purity of energy during the murdering, but this passed in moments. He watched all that he did now at an the indescribable distance deep in his head that was so far removed from what most people thought of as reality that in a sense he was traveling in a different time zone or dimension where nothing was real but rather a bizarre and often grotesque carnival ride. Humans were things to Miskis. Pieces on a chessboard of complex parameters. He was mostly detached from the physical world. His body went through the motions, but his mind worked its way through other dimensions, many of his own mental construction. He was keenly aware of this separation and being intelligent and cunning he was able to hold this duality together, keeping his madness in check or as he often thought "Keeping the sucker riding between the white lines." When he was finished violating his victims, he looted the bodies and went on his way. He'd lost count of how often he'd done this and didn't care anyway.

Over the years he not only had become good at his craft, he'd become skilled at living in the mountains or out on the high plains or remote desert areas like so many outcasts in this country. Anywhere is his home. He's learned the art of invisibility. Even at six-six with long hair and his full beard, he is able to walk down a street without attracting any notice. The secret he discovered is not being furtive or discreet, but rather moving through life erect, full of restrained confidence, never avoiding eye contact. Bore into them and scare them into forgetfulness. That is his trick and it always works. His internal force is too much for others and they quickly dismiss him from their minds. Few individuals embrace terror. They do whatever they can to avoid or erase from their lives the memory of this sensation. That's his secret, the reason he is able to do as he pleases and move about among people freely, without notice.

In the early eighties he bought a small cabin with a couple of rundown outbuildings on 80 acres up Indian Creek. His needs were basic - food, booze, very little sleep and some sex, which he satisfied during his robbery and murders, though these grew infrequent as time passed. He was moving towards a different line of work. He met the Omaha meat distributor in a bar one night in Ekalaka. He'd been down there poaching antelope not far from Ingomar and the distributor had been hunting on private-fee land. The two of them hit it off for some reason. Maybe it was because they both liked to drink whiskey and kill things. Maybe darkness is attracted to darkness. Doesn't really matter. As the years passed, Miskis and the man started doing business in wild game. Small doings at first, but by the time the Siksika's buffalo herd thing was in the final planning stages and about to come on line, both of them were making good money selling illegally-taken wild game. Most of the restaurants' owners or managers didn't care where the fish or elk or antelope came from as long as they were reassured that everything was on the up-and-up and pretty much legal. That they had the paperwork to back up the transactions. The guy from Omaha told them that the trout came from rivers and lakes in the West, all of the fish taken when a certain section of stream or a lake was netted prior to re-stocking or a big game herd was culled for the sake of population dynamics. No one with an ounce of sense really believed this, but the story had an environmentally-correct tone to it, and those involved were making a nice profit. So that was that. It was 1996. The buffalo herd manager was already a part of the deal, but Miskis was going to be stretched thin with the addition of the new angle. He needed a partner. Enter Mark Grace.

Miskis is in The Night Hawk kicking back a few quick ones before making the drive back to his cabin. He's come to town to pay past-due insurance premiums (play it straight with the small stuff that will bust you if you don't pay attention he always reasons) on the truck and house, buy groceries and booze, and pick up a couple of big-game hunting books he's ordered: *A Hunter's Wanderings in Africa – 1871-80* by F.C. Selous, *After Wild Sheep in Altai and Mongolia* by Prince Demidoff and *African Twilight* by Robert F. Jones. Miskis loves to read about real hunts by men who've really lived them. Somewhere in the back of his mind he's always wanted to be hunter, ever since that first hot, windy day when he first came to Montana, the time when the trucker let him off along the main drag in Miles City. On the drive up over the cracked concrete highway, this well before the homogenized and insane boredom served up by today's Interstates, he'd watched countless herds of antelope grazing among the hills and just below eroded ridgelines. Fat mule deer worked along dry, sandy washes, their huge heads and outrageous ears turning as they watched him pass by. Bands of antelope bounded and raced across parched sage flats, their white rumps vanishing in the wavering distance. Something unknown, crazily wild called to him. The country. The animals wandering completely free in the miles of loneliness. He wanted to walk through the harsh, parched land, to push through thorny thickets and crawl over ground full of prickly pear cactus as he stalked this game. For whatever reason he never got that chance. Almost from birth his life aimed itself in the direction of a harsh reality and the knowledge that to stay alive brutality, coldness and stealth would be required traits for him, what many people who have much easier lives like to conveniently label as evil. Miskis didn't choose this. It just happened. There was never a conscious design to be what he is now, anymore than there was an awareness that all he really wanted was to be far out in honest, empty country without thought, tracking antelope and deer. Some of us never have a chance to realize our peaceful dreams and we do horrible things, not for any damn good reason other than to just keep on going, to make it through another severe day so that we can take on another one. That's the way it is. Events happen in a random series of hard, hurtful events that sometimes lead inexorably to a life of mean times. That is Miskis. While leafing through his new books in the calm dimness of the bar, the front door bangs open and a man only a few inches shorter than himself stands silhouetted in the bright afternoon glare.

"Set 'em up for all my good friends, Waukonda, my dear," says Mark Grace as he strolls into the familiar dimness of the bar, landing on the stool next to Miskis. Waukonda is known among the patrons as Mrs. Science. She has graduate degrees from Cal State Northridge in both quantum physics and mathematics. A doctorate in the latter. Two of her pet projects are working on complicated formulas that predict rogue waves in the deep ocean. Waves that appear normal until they act out of convention, out of linear time, and begin sucking energy from the two waves closest to them. She hypothesizes that the rogues will grow rapidly to 100 feet or more with correspondingly deep trenches in front and behind them.

She claims that these waves are responsible for many unexplained shipping disasters. The department head at Cal State ridicules and dismisses her theory, but a recent study by a colleague of NASA satellite photos taken over a two-week period turned up dozens of these waves in the middle of calm seas. In light of the recent devastation caused by Tsunamis in Indonesia the government's become very interested in her work, so interested in fact that she's received one-hundred thousand to continue her studies. She continues to work at the Night Hawk because she enjoys the people and likes to have an excuse to escape her smoky study, she's a Lucky Strike chain smoker, from time to time. The change of setting, the bar' so=called ambience, also clears her mind and helps with the work on her postulations. Her other project is furthering the work of Dr. John Davies who hypothesized that all life on earth is the result of random collisions with fecal matter that has been voided from alien spacecraft. Northridge is eagerly awaiting her thesis on this odious subject. She claims that reference materials and congruent studies have been hard to come by. Waukonda fits into the Biederbeck mix like a well-worn kid-leather, shooting glove. She's one of the crew. The place wouldn't be the same without her. The regulars like her so much that they've started a fund to send her to a plush stop-smoking spa in Sri Lanka, a location that is ideal for her wave research. They're raised a couple of grand and need another four to send her on her way, hopefully before the onset of deadly diseases related to smoking.

"And give this guy next to me two of whatever he's drinking and please keep 'em coming, my dear" says

Grace. "I'm real dry."

Waukonda shrugs and builds the drinks.

"From the looks of things, you've been working on that thirst some already." A speech for Miskis.

"Just getting started my man. I've had a great week of work and a even better day fishing the river. Life is good right now and I want to make the most of the rest of this day with all of you."

Normally Miskis will either walk out or turn off anyone who displays this level of familiarity in his presence, but something about Grace catches his attention. Perhaps it is the whiskey Grace puts away with ease or maybe, as is the case with all true predators, Miskis senses a weakness in this man, a predilection towards being led down a very dark path. His bluff and bluster is a clear sign to Miskis that he is insecure, perhaps fearful of much that life presents. The poaching is going well right now, but he needs and wants to expand the operation. The Omaha connection is interested in trout and really interested in what passes these days for free-ranging, wild buffalo. Miskis needs help. There is too much work. Too many details and tasks for him alone. None of this passes through his mind consciously. The plans resonate somewhere down beneath the surface. The force of this energy spurs him to action. Talking over their drinks, Miskis learns that Grace is both an accomplished woodsman and hunter, that he makes his money cutting timber in the area with someone called Sam Jones. Also, that Grace puts meat on his table through hunting and fishing and most importantly to Miskis, the real trigger in the about-to-be partnership, Grace is far behind on his bills because he's run into an ice-cold streak with the cards at his weekly high stakes, for this town anyway, poker game. The river card never seems to have his best interests at heart. Grace is philosophical about this. He knows that bad luck is part and parcel of Texas Hold 'em poker. But he was raised to pay his bills in a timely fashion. Being behind with his creditors, many of them long-time friends from as far back as East Side Elementary School, worries him a lot. He dwells on this constantly even though these friends know they'll be paid. Card playing the debts that usually go with it are a common situation in Montana. Unless things go completely haywire, no one gets too worked up about this. Still, Grace worries, loses sleep and is drinking a little more than he should right now. Losing money betting on weak cards is something Grace seems to be getting quite good at doing.

"If the right ship sailed by, one with good money on it, I hop aboard and ride the thing for all it's worth, buddy. Maybe all the way to the flaming darkness to hell," says Grace and he flashes his large sapphire ring, the one on his right middle finger, in the low light, catching his new acquaintance's eye.

"That's one fine looking stone. Sapphire?"

"Sure is. One of the purest ever found in Montana. Over three carats. My grandfather willed it to me," says Grace with obvious pleasure and pride. "Been wearing it ever since he passed away. I'd rather he was alive then be wearing this ring, though. Boy did we have some times hunting sharptails up around Malta, pheasants, too. And we used to fish for the big northerns in Fresno Reservoir each April. Caught 'em over thirty pounds sometimes.

Man, that was living."

"I know what you mean about all of that, and that's one fine ring."

In his mind Miskis already owned it, could see himself wearing it. And he picks up on something else. "The flaming darkness of hell." He likes that one, knows about that place firsthand. He laughs to himself, thinking 'Hang with me, buddy. I'll get you there and then some.'

One thing leads to another and eventually Grace is sitting in front of a wood stove in the kitchen of Miskis's cabin. A pint bottle of whiskey went back and forth between them on the drive up in Miskis's rig. They talked long into the night, until Grace drifts off. In the morning Miskis drives Grace back to town. Over the following days he stays in close contact. He's had found the one he needs to jack his business up a notch or two. Over the fall and winter months he eases the younger man into the poaching, stringing him along with loans and paying him cash for ever more daring and in the eyes of the law, egregious, acts of poaching. By spring Grace no longer knows or cares about what is right or wrong concerning killing wild animals. Miskis has him hypnotized on this front. Grace now owes him money, too. Quite a bit of it. Grace isn't a weak man, but Miskis is a very powerful one. He's been forced to grow strong, mean, and hard in order to survive his father's beatings and to be able to live with the fact that his mother had run away from their home with another man, an accordion player who worked at a roadside tavern back in Illinois. The musician lured her away with talk of love and promises of a grand life in Rockford, a factory city an hour to the north. For an accordion player he was a flashy dresser and he always had a thick roll of twenties in his hip pocket. The mother was looking for something, anything better than her life alone with her drunken husband. One snowy winter night she left for the bar where the accordion player was and never came back. Miskis was four and the beatings started that night when his father returned drunk and discovered his wife gone. No note. She never even packed any clothes, but the man knew she was gone for good. Drunken instincts. He'd dragged his son from his bed, pulled off his belt, and beat Miskis until the boy passed out from the pain and the horror. That was only the beginning of nine years of torment and torture. Miskis survived and he did so by turning cold and mean in a way that embraced the worst sort of beast that lives in all of us. Again, he would never have chosen this path. He was sucked down into it until cruelty and death seemed as natural to him as laughter and kindness do to most of the rest humanity. So hypnotizing Grace, getting him in tow, is nothing for this man, who has brutalized and killed more people than he can easily remember. Why should he? Other humans are nothing to him other than a means to an end. When he sliced off his father's head, he also cut the last tenuous connection he had with the rest of his species.

As Bouchee's truck rattles away out of sight, Miskis laughs at how easy sucking Grace into all of this has been. "All of them are nothing. They have no wills. Moving them around is almost boring. Childish tricks is all. Nothing more." This said aloud to no one. Miskis backs out of the creek and walks silently back to his cabin a couple of miles away over a timbered ridge.

~ ~ ~

The morning after talking with Dirt at the bar I wake up to a ringing phone. I decide to let the answering machine deal with. And I also rise to the crashing roar of a thunderstorm. There's been no rain for over a week, only the threat of some. Every afternoon small clouds will build into larger ones that eventually towered thousands of feet above their dark, turbulent bases and hold over the spiked tops of the surrounding mountains. Apparently today sufficient moisture and static electricity has gathered for this downpour. Already well after sunrise, but the street lights are still on, broadcasting distorted reflections in the wet pavement. The light appears unnatural, eerie at this hour of the day creating an uncomfortable sensation similar to an eclipse of the sun in early afternoon. Rain is pounding on the streets and being plastered sideways in waves by fierce gusts of wind. The smell of ozone is thick, even inside, reminding me of walking through a hospital hallway to the emergency room. The drumming of the drops on parked cars and trucks makes it impossible to hear the forecast on The Weather Channel, but today's map shows clear skies and only a 10 percent chance for precipitation. The pregnant weather girls – they always seem to be with child on that network, one of life's little mysteries – smile and say to enjoy a beautifully clear summer day out in Montana. A blinding flash is followed immediately by a clap of thunder that rattles the coffee cup on my dusk. Even The Dog wakes up. This continues for awhile, then the mayhem seems to move away to the east. I'm wrong. Pea sized hail begins dinging off of everything. It grows larger. To marble size, then becomes the diameter of quarters. From the window I watch as windshields crack and auto bodies dent in the onslaught. What was loud before is deafening now, especially with the new salvos of lightning and thunder. I turn around to see how all this noise is affecting canine ears. The Dog's not around. I walk through the apartment searching and finally find him huddled in a ball in the bathtub, curtain drawn.

"It's okay buddy. It will pass."

I stroke his curled form. He shudders uncontrollably. I pet him some more. He looks at me with wide eyes and then quickly hides his head again. I cover him with a large bath towel and walk back to my desk. The storm is cooling out some so I press the replay button on the answering machine.

"Ed, this is Liz Jones. When you get a chance, would you please call me and tell me what you've found out so far." She thanked me or rather my machine for my time and left her number. I was going over to the police station to talk to Qualls around nine to see if he'd turned up anything, but I dial Liz's number and arrange to meet with her at eleven. She sounds upbeat and eager to talk.

Since the bathtub is occupied, I pass on a shower, get dressed and stroll out the back door headed for the cop shop, that is next to a big, old brick school that is now a fly fishing museum. The pursuit is taken seriously around here. Some of the finest trout streams anywhere are located within a hundred-mile radius of Biederbeck. Some good lakes, too. Maybe a couple thousand hiding out in the mountains and out on the prairie if you count ranch and beaver ponds. Rainbows, cutthroat, browns, brook trout, even goldens abound in the region, not to mention mountain whitefish by the zillions, grayling, northern pike and some small and largemouth bass. A nexus for fly fishers from all over the world including presidents that have included Carter, Eisenhower and Hoover. A number of top-quality fly shops employ an assortment of guides possessing a vast range of skills, dispositions and drift boats. Most of the guides are competent and many of the drift boats are safe. The museum itself has hundreds of old bamboo fly rods built and fished by the greats and not-so-greats, antique reels, displays of old and new fly patterns, mounts of huge trout that probably came from some meat market located near the Great Lakes, photos of the those very same greats standing in a river or holding nearly dead fish, and there are tanks of live trout swimming sadly around in perpetual circles in confined discouragement. These fish interest me the most. I'm sure if they can see through the glass of their prisons. Most of the time when I tap my finger on the sides or, when no one's looking, press my face to the cold glass, the trout remain motionless, suspended in the water. Every now and then, one will give a lazy flick of its fins and glide over to me and then hang suspended again for a long time, the only movement is the steady pulsing of fins and tails as it maintains position in front of my face. I feel sorry for these trout. To some extent I empathize with their confinement having been through a similar horror years ago when I worked on a small daily newspaper up in the northwest corner of the state. The managing editor was a former third grade teacher, not bad in of itself, but when coupled with a massive ego fueled by insecurity stemming from the fact that he and his entire staff knew he was not qualified for the position, my job as a reporter became a miserable experience. Memos, changes in policy, back stabbing, the editor's nick-name was "Black Dan," all of it created a scene that I was mercifully fired from when I showed up to work three days straight more than a little bit intoxicated. I certainly could have handled things better, but I'd come to the paper after working on another in Wisconsin for a couple of years. A paper that had a real managing editor, a top-flight editorial staff and all that went with this. The change from a serious paper to an advertising rag was abrupt, unexpected and depressing. So I understood how these fish felt, if they indeed felt anything. Hell, even if they're hatchery bred and reared, they deserve their freedom and the opportunity that is their birthright to take their chances against larger fish, mammalian and avian predators, pollution and the never-ending assortment of flies, hardware, garlic-flavored marshmallows and frozen bullheads that pound the state's waters. How will these fish ever know what living really was unless they taste a thick, juicy night crawler or a piece of Nibblets canned corn. Their situation seems most unjust to my way of thinking. They belong in the Hart or the Jefferson or the Madison, even the hopelessly over-fished Bitterroot in the southwestern corner of the state. Not here.

The entrance to the station is next to the museum. Qualls' office is in the back. I say hello to Ginny who is manning the front desk, spot Jim at his desk. Ginny's reading a tattered copy of Graham Greene's *A Burnt-out Case*. She looks up, smiles, waves me on and returns to her book. I walk in. The room is about fifteen-by-fifteen with two windows that look out on a parking lot and the wall of the old school's gym, which is now a combination thrift shop and senior citizens' center. The bricks have been painted by some of the town's local talent with a group of ballerinas in various positions as they silently perform for the wind, rain, sun and stray road bum wandering by on his way to the Humble Heart soup kitchen. The walls of Qualls' office are covered with hunting photos, pictures of Qualls holding the head of a just-killed antelope, elk, mule deer, whitetail or bear. And there's one of a sheep he shot in the mountains surrounding Faro, Yukon taken years ago when he used to hunt big game all over the globe. These days he confines his hunting to Montana. And there were lots of shots of him and his hunting buddies hoisting heavy strings of ducks, pheasants and handfuls of upland birds. He even has a snapshot where he looks like he's strangling a huge sandhill crane with both hands by the throat. The bird is nearly as long as he is tall. I shake my head. Hunting in this state is serious business. I'm at most a dilettante in this area. He's reading an old copy of *The New Yorker*.

Looking up he exclaims "You gotta read this story by Annie Proulx. Unbelievable. It's about two young guys who spend the summer in the Wyoming mountains guarding a herd of sheep. You can't believe the stuff they do. Unbelievable," and he sets down the magazine, lights his pipe and takes a hit of cop shop coffee. "Want a cup?"

What the hell? Life is to be lived to its fullest. I go out and pour a mug of the blackest, thickest, ugliest coffee ever made, and don't forget, I've been married to someone who hated me, still does if her last phonecall six months ago means anything. Going for it all, I pass on sugar and cream and take a healthy swallow of the brew straight.

"Good God, Qualls! This is awful, even by this place's standards. What in the hell is in here?"

"Irene put some salt in the pot this morning. Said she read in a gourmet magazine that it improves the flavor," he says taking another sip. "I tend to agree."

"I've heard that, too, but only a pinch. Did she say how much she put in?"

"I watched her make it this morning when I came in. She added two tablespoons with a pound of coffee. That's seems about right, for me anyway."

The liquid was bitter, salty and loaded with caffeine. I ask how large the pot is and Qualls says he thinks a dozen cups. All things considered, two tablespoons seem appropriate. I'll battle my way through this cup, but that's it. Like I said earlier, you really have to live here for awhile to appreciate some of this stuff. There's no single thing that makes Biederbeck unique or even a touch strange. It's more a combination of thousands of tiny. Seemingly insignificant, incidents that form a sum much greater than the parts. Say, for instance this coffee, Ginny reading Graham Greene, a copy reading *The New Yorker,* the ballet tableau and on and on. It's more a matter of the insanely, relentless series of these things, day after day, never letting up. Seventy-year-old men with long-gray ponytails riding motorized skateboards along the levee next to the river, Happy Hour at Ray's, giant trout pulling a painter into the river, a flock of over one-thousand non-migratory geese that make the town their home and walking a sporting proposition on several levels. The place's most famous fly tier earned his stripes when he invented a pattern called the Bugger Duck, a combination of duct tape and white or yellow marabou. Best damn streamer I've ever used. His photo along with a writer friend of his, the pair holding a brace of twenty-plus-inch browns they'd taken the day of the pattern's inception, hang on the wall of the Round the Bend Bar, along with an assortment of other slightly odd portraits of local anglers. My picture sitting next to the dog, both of us perched on bar stools, also graces the walls of the venerable establishment.

A strong spell of dizziness makes me forget why I'm here in the first place. Damn good coffee. I recover and buzz on over to the chair in front of the desk, passing the chief on his way out to the pot for another cup, one I notice that he loads down with thick cream and lots of sugar. Anybody could drink this crud that way. A little Beam probably would work as well. He sits down and looks at me.

"Heard from Dirt that you were up to Indian Creek and that you found a tail from a buffalo."

I reach into my coat pocket, grab the stub and toss the thing to him. He turns it over in his hands, before dropping it on the magazine. "Probably means nothing. Mere coincidence. Awkward incidence," and he smiles in a strange way. Whatever this Biederbeck craziness is, it never stops around here. Awkward incidence?

"Dirt doesn't think so. He said the tail is the key to the murder. He usually homes in pretty well on these things," and I choke down some more salty coffee.

"You might be right. I heard from Jones's doctor yesterday and apparently he's obsessed with doing pencil drawings of buffalo or as I'm told he says over and over 'Actually they're bison,' whatever the Sam hell that means." Qualls pauses then laughs. "Not a bad pun all things considered." He laughs some more. "The only buffalo or bison I know of around here are up in the park and they've been behaving themselves aside from the random charge at the odd tourist, and wandering out and getting shot" and he just smiles this time. 'I've got nothing new. How 'bout you?"

"No, not really. I did find a small piece of skin that I thought was probably Grace's. It's still up there by the fire ring, if the ants or magpies haven't eaten it by this time."

"We found plenty enough and it all matched with Grace. No big deal." Montana casual, cop style. Qualls is a good cop. Conscientious, honest, caring. He'd worked vice in Billings for 11 years and that was not easy time. Billings is filled with oil money and all of the drugs, hookers, booze, violence and weirdness that comes with it. When the chance to return to his hometown opened up after the previous sheriff died of a heart attack. One brought on when he was discovered by his wife screwing his secretary on the desk Qualls is sitting behind now, well, Qualls leaped at the chance. In the following seven years he's managed to keep Biederbeck on a relatively even keel and is doing this with a patient, reasonable hand. He believes in the spirit of the law, not the letter. And a number of us have avoided jail time and big fines because of this man's easy-going approach to law enforcement. Instead of public intoxication charges or unlawful firing of firearms within city limits, he's talked us down to a modest level of lunacy and defused the situations that are forgotten with the sun rise of the next day. On the other side of the coin, if there is serious trouble or someone truly gets out of hand, Qualls deals with the situation immediately, severely and with no b.s. He's a good cop and an even better friend. He's one of my fishing and hunting buddies. We've spent many hours wading streams chasing trout or working side hill grouse covers in deep coulees up by Fairfield or as far east as Circle.

So, that's the end of that line of conversation for the moment. We waste a few minutes talking trout and fly fishing before I get up to leave.

"Bouchee, take this with you, I don't need it." He flips the tail to me. I miss the play and have to pick it up from the floor. "Good hands."

"Always a pleasure, Jim. Talk to you in a few days and thanks for the coffee. Damn good," and I zip out of the place, the caffeine making my feet slide across the floor in a spastic rhythm. I hear Ginny laughing as I leave. So what? I need some fresh air and a cigarette.

I stop for breakfast at a diner on the way back, scrambled eggs, fried calf brains, cinnamon roll, and orange juice. By the time I open the front door Liz is already there, sitting on the couch holding the dog's head in her lap. He looks pathetic, moon-eyed. I wonder where he gets it. Liz looks great. Hair shining. Face rosy. White cotton blouse and tight jeans adding to the picture. No way around it, she was a fine-looking woman. I sit down behind my desk and light another smoke. I decide to pass on the coffee for now. Liz already has a mug of her own. She settles back into the couch. The Dog doesn't move a muscle. He knows when life is sweet and rides it for all it was worth.

"Does he have a name or is he just The Dog?" She asks as she plays with his ears, stretching them out and gently smoothing them on her lap. Something to be said here for big ears.

"Never could think of a name that suited him. The Dog seems to work fine for both of us."

"How do call you him? Here The Dog. Come here The Dog? That sounds odd to me."

"Never have to. When I want him to come or wonder where he is, he shows up. The little guy never strays very far and he always knows when we're going somewhere or, like all dogs, when the possibility of food exists. I swear he reads my mind. Makes things easy."

"I bet he does. Probably isn't much work for him anyway."

She laughs at her shot at me, a merry, open sound. Delightful. Turning to what passes for business in my life, I fill Liz in on my talks with Dirt and Qualls, and about my trip to Indian Creek. When I mention the buffalo tail her eyes go wide up briefly with a look of recognition or understanding, but she quickly moves on, subtly redirecting the conversation by rambling on and on about Sam's drawings and his repetition of the line "Actually they're bison," and how isn't life riddled with coincidence.

"Dirt really thinks there's something to the tail. I know I said I didn't think my looking into the matter would lead anywhere, but something about all of this, for lack of a better word, intrigues me, so I'm going to stay with it for awhile," I say. "If nothing comes of any of my efforts, I'll bill you for my time and expenses up to now. The rest is on me. Okay?"

Liz looks out the window with a distant not really in the same room gaze, then turns to me and smiles. "Yes. That's very kind of you. And generous, but don't waste too much of your time on this damn buffalo tail. Dirt may be wrong. There's probably nothing here. I'm almost sure of it. The thing being up there is probably just an odd deal and that's nothing new around here."

I have to admit she has a point on that one. Normal is a relative term in the best of situations. In Biederbeck the word can and often does mean anything.

"I'll be out of town until Friday. I have some things to take care of and getting away from here and all of this will help clear my head and calm me down so I can make better decisions about what needs to be done. I'll call when I get back."

She gently removes The Dog's head from her lap, stands up and walks over to the coffee pot where she sets down her mug. "This is only a mild suggestion, but it might be a good idea to wash all of this," and she looks at the stained table top, the grungy pot, the off-white cups and dull spoons, "in very hot, soapy water," and she laughs, a buoyant, cheery sound, flashing dark, shining eyes my way.

"See you soon," and she glides out the door and out of view.

An attractive woman in so many ways, I think. Funny and energetic. I pick up the buffalo tail and turn it over and over in my hands. Nothing here, she said. I'm not so sure about that.

~ ~ ~

Miskis is waiting for her at the shed when she pulls up. He heard the Landcruiser lugging up the dirt road to his place and saw the thin cloud of dust rising behind it from the kitchen window. Liz parks the rig inside. He slides the large shed door shut behind them. They walk quickly to the cabin. Once inside, out of view, they embrace sharing a passionate, wild kiss, then he picks her up and carries her into the bedroom where they make love quickly the first time. They've not been together for long weeks. The next time is slower, though equally intense as they concentrate on giving each other pleasure, both enjoying the long ride. When they were finish, Miskis goes into the kitchen and pours them each a glass of whiskey. Returning with the bottle, he hands a glass to her and lights a cigarette, which they share in silence while sipping their drinks.

"God, it seems like forever since ..." and she trails off. "I've missed you like crazy and have been going nuts. Lord only knows why. Never say a nice thing to me. Hardly talk at all. You've got me hypnotized. I have no control over myself any more."

She looks up at him. He returns the gaze saying nothing. She thinks about the time she first met this closed, secretive man and how a lot of little things have combined to lead them to here, to right now. Grace is dead. Her husband most likely is forever insane. The possibility of two of them going to prison is not all that far away.

Sam and Mark were longtime friends and earned a fair living together cutting timber on national forest sales around the state, mainly in The Hart drainage of the Nortons, though when the stumpage fee was right, they had ranged as far away as the Custer National Forest in the southeastern corner of the state. Over the years she grew close to Mark and considered him a friend, of sorts. They'd spent hundreds of hours talking about their pasts, their families, their dreams and day-to-day issues. He'd always been there when Sam was in one of his infrequent low moods, periods when he grew silent and withdrew into himself. These bouts with depression lasted only a couple of days, three at the most, but they felt like months to Liz. Hour upon hour of silence, Sam never looking at her. And he never slept when he was like this. By the time the lack of rest pushed him to mania, talking to himself, pacing the house, drinking way too much, Liz was a basket case herself. She would hold on as long as she could but finally out of desperation she'd call Mark and he'd be at the back door in minutes. He was aware of Sam's moods and kept a discreet eye on things, staying in the background waiting for her call. Snapping Sam out of it wasn't so much his doing, but more a function of timing. When Sam reached the point of near madness, he was almost home, he'd almost worked his way through whatever dark incident in his past was tormenting him.

This usually involved something dealing with his parents' divorce (ugly, protracted and at times violent) when he was little or his father disinheriting him because he chose to be a logger in Montana instead of going to the University of Michigan and following in his father's footsteps by becoming a lawyer. This wasn't for him - the regular hours in an office, the constricting suit and tie, the public exposure of trying a case in court, all of it; and trying to cope with the hideous social niceties like belonging to a pretentious country club, entertaining partners who were as miserable as he was, marrying a trophy wife. None of this was for Sam. He termed it a "long-running. Stylized death trip." He'd decided early on that he preferred, even needed, the openness and freedom of the mountains and high plains of Montana and the freedom of working as his own boss as a private contractor logger even though the money wasn't often good and the work was brutal and dangerous. He'd first visited Montana on a family vacation to the Gallatin Valley when he was thirteen. From the first morning when he awoke to the sight of mountains rising in the clear, cold air, the blue trout streams, the wild smell of the sage flats, the elk grazing on a far hill, Sam knew he'd found home. The worst aspects of his life in Montana struck him as being a whole lot better than anything associated with becoming an attorney. His father had ceased to speak with him when Sam moved west from Oak Park, Illinois and the family home. When his father died from lung cancer years ago all Sam received was a box of old clothes, another box of Alcoholics Anonymous books and brochures, and a copy of the legal codicil in his father's will that stated that he'd receive some of the vast wealth his father had accumulated from practicing law, investing in local cable TV providers in the Midwest, buying television and radio stations and real estate around the country when he turned fifty or was incapacitated by injury or illness. Sam was seven years from fifty. His health was excellent. No money in a big box looming on the near horizon. The lack of inheritance didn't bother him, except for the fact that his father had written Sam from his life and after his death. He could never figure out or understand why his father hated him because he refused to become a lawyer and instead chose a path that appealed to him. He'd never relied on anyone for money. He took care of his own bills, debts and acquisitions. Sam was never able to walk away from the hurt caused by his father's intractable, self-centered, behavior. When this pain became too much, he'd drift off within himself and only he could bring himself back. That's just the way it was and always would be he'd tell Liz and Mark when he'd return from his private hell.

So, at these times of the blues with Sam, all Mark really had to do was show up, sit Liz's husband down and start retelling things the two of them had done in the past, make him start laughing. Like the time they were in Chicago taking in a Cubs-Cardinals four-game series and they'd wound up downtown very drunk vainly trying to hail a cab to take them somewhere to eat. Sam stood in the middle of Rush street, hand raised with his index pointed skyward. Cars veered around him, horns blaring and obscenities flying. Finally a cabbie stopped and said he would take them anywhere as long as it was on the way through the North Side. It was the end of the day and he was heading home. They climbed in and told the driver to take them to anyplace that served great food. He dropped them off on Wells Street in Old Towne, not far from the ballpark they'd left a few hours earlier. He pointed to an old brick building across the street. "Best steaks in the city and a spinach soufflé that is out of this world." The two thanked the man, tipped him twenty bucks and walked into the place. The maitre de was less than impressed with their appearance, but condescended to seat them in the back near the door to the kitchen. Busy and noisy, but what the hell? They were hungry. They ordered New York strips rare and the spinach, and told the obsequious waiter, whose name was Paul, but they kept calling Maurice, to bring them a round of Heinekens and shots of Jack Daniels and to deliver the same every time he passed by. When the food arrived they were both roaring drunk, but managed to eat their steaks with knives and forks. The soufflé did not fair quite so well. They ate this delicacy and some fluffy potatoes with their fingers, drawing a certain amount of aghast attention from both the staff, and the clientele, who did their best to enjoy their meals all the while praying that these two lunatics would leave soon without becoming violent. For some reason, perhaps a fortuitous, simple twist of fate, the management did forgo calling the gendarmes. Lucky for them. A night in the Cook County Jail can be an eye-opening experience. When they were finished they both stood up simultaneously, wiping spinach from their hands on the table cloth. Silver and dishware clattered to the floor, pieces of busted china careering far and wide. The place went silent. They were the center of outraged attention. Noticing this, with the exaggerated aplomb of the hopelessly smashed, they each pushed a pair of twenties in the waiter's shirt pocket with a grand flourish, patted the terrified man heartily on the back saying "Tremendous service Maurice, you old fart," paid the bill up front, wandered outside and somehow managed to find their way back downtown to their truck buried in a subterranean parking lot beneath Michigan Avenue. Sam and Mark had dozens of amusing anecdotes like this in their past. They bored their friends silly telling them.

Once his friend had Sam's attention, telling a few of these tales would snap Liz's husband out of his grim demeanor, even if he was drunk, but you had to wait until Sam reached terminal velocity for this to work. Any sooner, and he would stare through Mark, go sulk in the bedroom or leave abruptly staggering out the door and wander the neighborhood for hours. Neither Liz nor Mark knew what triggered or led to the boiling point that precipitated these emotional swings. Sam could not explain what led to critical mass in this area, dusting the miserable episodes off with "Sometimes all of it becomes too much for me. I get blue and can't climb out of it for awhile."

'For awhile,' Liz thinks as she watches Miskis pour each of them another drink. Try for god-damned eternity. This man is different. Much different. He doesn't say much, but he is always with her, always there for her mentally, spiritually, and physically even when they are apart. He fills a void in Liz that she's dragged along with her all her life. Even his solid, tangible darkness is better, far better, than being so far alone she often feels like she was wandering through a dream that never ends. With Miskis she feels connected to something, alive. He's dark, frightening, bordering on evil but a creature filled with untamed, wild energy that sweeps over her in ceaseless waves intoxicating her in ways she's never experienced or imagined before. There are times when his powerful hold on her makes her do things that she can't remember doing, that she'd never do on her own. 'It's voodoo or hypnotism,' she often says to herself, but she's addicted and unable to pull away from what she intrinsically knows is very wrong. She feels like what she imagines a heroin addict must feel like – high on his drug and totally hooked, lost, addled, twitching as hell without it. Her fix is Miskis. She can't get enough of him or what he offers her.

She loves Sam. Wants the best for him. She considers Bouchee her friend and truly appreciates everything he's doing for her, but she's obsessed with Miskis. On one level or another or on many levels he's always with her. The need to be with him physically, to have as much of him as she can absorb, is ever present dictating and driving her thoughts and actions. She knows she is doing bad, harmful things to herself and most importantly in her mind, to others. Yet, she can't help herself and is more and more often thinking "I don't care about any of this being wrong. I'm alive when I'm with him. I don't care about any of the rest of it any more.'

Six years ago this month Mark came over to the house one night extremely excited, almost agitated, about someone he'd met in The Night Hawk. A guy called Thomas Miskis who loved to hunt and fish and knew how to live in the woods just like him and Sam. He went on and on about all the things this Miskis did, like stalking elk for hard miles in the high country, shooting the animal, quartering it and then hauling the heavy chunks of elk for those same miles down through dense timber, swampy terrain and over deadfalls. Or how he would wade a large river like the Missouri in a December blizzard casting weighted streamers for hours searching for huge brown trout. Fishing for hours, sometimes never connecting with a fish. Things like that. Later on, after she'd gotten to know

Miskis some, Liz wondered about all of the tales. Not just fact that she'd never seen or even heard him talk about any hunting or fishing, but the basic fact that she'd never heard him put more than two sentences together in all the time she spent with him, which was considerable, especially during the last three years.

A few weeks after this, Mark arranged for all of them to get together for drinks at The Mint Bar in White Sulphur Springs, a small ranching town eighty miles north of Biederbeck. Sam and Mark were logging a sale in the Pinnacle Mountains outside of town and would come in every couple of days for dinner and drinks. Mark bumped into Miskis the week before while topping off the truck at a local service station. The two agreed to meet the next Friday night with Sam and Liz. Liz agreed in a conversation with Sam and said that she would drive up for the night. She was missing her husband and reserved a room at a hotel in the area.

When she walked into the bar that evening the three men were already seated at a table by the door. Mark stood up and introduced Miskis to Liz. He never moved and only said "It's a pleasure," but when he said those three words, she experienced a thrill she hadn't felt in years with Sam. It felt like a strong jolt of adrenaline rushing through her veins instantly opening and expanding her. The man's deep voice cut deeply, right to the heart, but nothing like his eyes. Two coal black lights beamed hard into her soul. Miskis at once scared and excited her. They drank and talked well into the night, forgetting all about dinner. Mark and Sam spoke excitedly about the upcoming big-game season, not noticing that Miskis never took his eyes off Liz. She tried to avoid eye contact with him, but even when talking with the other two or sipping her drink, she could feel the force of this silent man's gaze on her. The few times she looked over at him, he never blinked, never moved his head. She felt like she was being hypnotized by Miskis (a feeling she would grow quite familiar with as time passed), and was excited by the danger he radiated, excited to an extreme she was unfamiliar with. Her hands shook and her vision wavered. Her heart pounded and went through a series of disquieting palpitations. Near closing Sam said it was time for him and Liz to head to their motel room. Mark offered a bubbly "See the two of you in the morning for breakfast." Miskis nodded in Sam's direction, but he kept his focus on the woman. He hadn't said more than a few words all night. Later when she was making love with Sam, she was thinking of Miskis. What was it about him that pulled her his way? He didn't say anything, but she found him fascinating. She knew that he was trouble for her and for her husband. Her instincts went off the chart on this, screaming warnings to stay away from this stranger. Stay away. She attempted to drive his image from her mind. When Sam was done, she turned over and tried to sleep.

She began to dose off, to drift away, but as soon as she did, the dark eyes of Miskis appeared. Then his hawk-like nose. Then the mouth filled with large white teeth, and then the long hair and beard. The image of his face was sharply defined like a negative of a photograph, only instead of being in shades of gray, this one was in deep maroon with an even darker background. The color of blood she thought and she opened her eyes again. She finally fell asleep near dawn dreaming chaotic dreams that she was unable to recall when she awoke later in the morning. All she was sure of was that life had changed for her last night and nothing would ever look or feel the same again. She felt uneasy and worried about her future with Sam. About all of their futures.

In the following weeks Liz was unable to keep Miskis from of her thoughts. While Sam and Grace worked at finishing with their cutting up north, she busied herself with completing magazine assignments for environmental magazines like *OnEarth and E*, which she found ironically humorous considering the fact that her husband was a logger, a profession anathema to both publications. She also took long walks in the sage-covered hills around Coltrane. One afternoon as she walked back home down the gravel road that led to the highway she spotted a pickup coming towards her, pushing up a rise. As it came closer she saw Miskis behind the wheel. She recognized the feelings of fear and sensual frenzy that raced through her stomach. It was the way she felt at The Mint that night. He pulled up alongside her, rested his arms on the steering wheel, not saying a word, only looking at her through the passenger window. "God, does he ever talk?" she wondered, but she wasn't afraid of this man. Only excited and, she admitted to herself, aroused.

Finally she managed to ask "Yes?" That's all she could manage.

He leaned over, opened the door and she got in. She sat in his truck, shut the door and that was all there was to it. Something she would never have considered doing with someone she barely knew like this mysterious man. Liz was gently, but firmly drawn into this man's truck, like being sucked way down deep by a powerful whirlpool. He turned around right there in the road and headed to the highway where he headed north for about twenty miles, before turning off on the Indian Creek road. Forty minutes later the truck veered off on a dirt lane that wound through easy draws and crossed a small creek, eventually climbing up over a grassy hill to a split-log cabin sheltered by thick-trunked Ponderosa pines. Beyond this the peaks of the Nortons cut high against the sky, their sheer rock massif dominating a large portion of the horizon. "Beautiful" she said aloud. Miskis parked near a shed. Killed the engine, got out and started walking for the cabin. Liz sat there. She heard a door open, boot steps on wooden steps and sounds of walking across the floor inside.

"Jesus what have I gotten myself into?"

She sat perfectly still for a long time. The sun was starting to set. The air was turning cool. She climbed out of the truck and walked through the cabin door. She never even thought about it. She simply got out and walked inside Miskis's cabin.

He was sitting at a round wooden table in the middle of the kitchen. A kerosene lantern cast a yellow-orange glow. A fire was popping and crackling in an old Majestic wood stove. A chair directly opposite him was pulled back for her. A glass of something, probably whiskey, was there waiting. He sat with his arms crossed on his lap. A cigarette was burning in an ashtray. She looked around. Everything was wood, the floor, walls, ceiling. No paintings or pictures anywhere. The place was clean and tidy. Blue enamel cookware and plates were neatly stacked on the counter between the stove and the sink. Through the crack in one open door she could see a bathroom. Through another was a living room with a stone fireplace and a couch in front of it. No rugs, but plenty of books stacked around the couch and on a table next to it. She noticed a copy of Jack London's *Daughter of the Snows* resting on the couch. She could read the faded title and see the design of the arcing aurora and trees pressed into the cloth in red and white.

"Maybe a first addition," she said.

"It is," he said startling her because she thought she'd kept this observation to herself, didn't speak aloud.

A kerosene lantern was burning here, too. A fire had been laid in the hearth. 'Not a lot of windows or light, but not gloomy, either,' she thought and then almost laughed out loud as she realized that she might be raped or murdered or God only knows what else by this man who says nothing and 'I'm standing here critiquing his decor.' The weirdest part of this was that now she still felt no fear or apprehension but rather a sense of familiarity and ease. She walked over, sat down and pulled a cigarette from his pack. He remained motionless. She lit the thing with a stick match she fumbled out from a box on the table, inhaled deeply, blew the smoke out and downed the whiskey in her glass. She never did this either. She liked to sip her drinks. The notion of gulping a couple of ounces of liquor in one take was not her style, but then being around Miskis made everything seem different and new in a out-of-focused familiar way.

He poured her another drink. The two remained

sitting in silence for a long time looking at each other. Normally when people stared at her she grew uncomfortable, but with him it was different. She was drawn into his eyes and she didn't resist. She kept coming to him. Their two lives, who they were, was coming out of them and mixing in the soft light above the lantern. She could see a silver-blue glow, one that grew and rose up through the beamed ceiling, and she could now see this ethereal light spreading and rising in the night sky, connecting with distant stars - not really thoughts or even emotions, but something that cut right to the heart of their beings, who she was and who he was. This was the substance of the light. She was still Liz, more so, but she was becoming Miskis, and he was merging with her. She could actually feel who he was and she sensed that the same thing was taking place in him, not within them, but in the space across the table between them, spinning above the lantern. Everything in the cabin except Miskis was gone. And then he was standing beside her and lifting her in his arms, carrying her weightless body through space into another room where he placed her down and undressed her. He took off his clothes. And they were together. For a long time. But when she next looked around, she was back in her home, lying in her own bed. Nothing looked the same or felt the way she imagined she remembered it. All of her past was still there, but all of the events and feelings no longer meant anything to her. They were like photographs of someone else's life. Nothing in her life was as it used to be. She thought of Sam and the love, friendship and loyalty still remained within her but like a washed out photograph with little definition or intensity of color.

Miskis had done this to her without words. He was all there was. That's how she wanted the remainder of her life to be.

From that point on, her life was Miskis. She was rarely with him physically, but in other ways she was at his side. She went about going through the motions of her life in Coltrane, around Biederbeck, with her friends and with Sam as though nothing had changed, but she was always with this dark man in spirit and in her mind. When she closed her eyes she saw him. When she dreamed, he was there. He was all she thought of. The other part of her life was now a meaningless dance and always would be. Liz believed that even if she were to die right this instant, she would still be with him. Maybe she was right. It no longer mattered and no one noticed her change. She remained married on paper to Sam, but lived for Miskis. No, she was a part of him know. The merger was complete. She could no longer discern the difference between the two of them. She moved through these worlds simultaneously with ease and fluidity.

And time passed.

She recalled all of this the instant when he looked over at Miskis. He was sitting up turning one of those damned buffalo tail stubs over and over in his hands.

"Those damn things are going to get us in trouble. Even Bouchee, the PI that I hired for show, is on to it. He found one near Mark's grave and he's already talked about it to the cops and others in town, damnit," and she grew angry as he kept his back to her. "Well you please say something, anything?"

He turned around and stared at her. Then he took her by the shoulders and rolled her onto her stomach.

~ ~ ~

Sam's doctor called me that morning and asked if I could drive over to Turbid Spring. Liz had visited the facility yesterday. She told him that I was working for her investigating Mark's murder. She also mentioned this to Sam, who said nothing for close to an hour while working on another drawing in his extensive buffalo suite.

Liz sat there watching him sketch, when out of the blue he turned to her and said "Actually it's bison. Bouchee knows what I'm talking about. Bring him on down. Yes, by all means, bring him on down. And actually it's bison." He then turned away and started another drawing.

Liz left the room and reported what had just happened to the shrink. The two of them went back to Sam's room and this time all he said was "Bring him on down." They assumed Sam meant me, so here I am driving down a cottonwood-lined road that leads to the state mental hospital, hoping to find out God only knows what. There've been times when I was reasonably convinced that if I didn't reign in my behavior or adopt a more positive attitude about life that I'd be spending some time in this place, hopefully on their *Extended Stay Discount Option*. The place is huge and looks like a prison, which in a way it is. The walls rise four stories and are made from large blocks of rectangular granite. The building is at least three-hundred-feet-long with wings at either end running a couple of hundred more feet behind. The grounds are enclosed by a high fence rimmed with shiny silver razor-wire. I must pass inspection at the front gate. The guard, no doubt highly-trained, reeks of Carlo Rossi's finest vintage. He glances at my driver's license and PI license before dropping my wallet on the pavement as he attempts to return it to me. He bends over. No easy task in his intoxicated condition and with his enormous gut worshipping its great god gravity, picks it up, winches himself upright with his face now beet red, hands it to me and totters off to the guard house, florid face beaming in the sunlight. I drive another quarter-mile and park next to an ambulance. I get out of the truck and walk through the large double doors and up to the front desk, my boots make a hollow sound that reverberates around the reception area, for lack of a better word to describe the cold, bleak space. I give my name and ask to see Sam's doctor, Walt Moryn, and add that I'm expected. The receptionist punches a button on her phone, speaks briefly and says "Wait here" to me. Looking around I can see that the place is old but has recently undergone some renovation. There are new tile floors and white paint. Lots of it. The sun shining through large windows reflects off the walls and ceiling and its intensity hurts my eyes. There are no chairs to sit in while I wait. Even the dentist gives me a place to sit and cower in fear while I pretend to read fourteen-year-old copies of People Magazine, Modern Maturity and Redbook.

The last time I'd been in a mental hospital was over twenty-five years ago when I worked as an orderly on a crisis unit at a similar place, only this one was located in northern Wisconsin, near a town called Minocqua. They paid me eighty bucks a week to snitch on the patients or clients as the staff preferred to call them. The inmates were always doing something heinous such as getting someone to smuggle in a six-pack of Chief Oshkosh beer or a Playboy. Terrible things like that. I also became quite skilled at ping-pong and the fine art of adjusting the score to suit the tempo of the game and the ever-fluctuating demeanor of my opponent. And a big part of my job was making sure that everyone really did swallow their medication instead of rolling the pills and tablets under their tongues to be hoarded for future festivities, usually on the occasion of a full moon. When a patient I liked lost it in front of me one day and ran straight through a full-length thermal-pane window screaming the words to "Mystic Eyes," an old song by a group called Them, I'd had enough. Especially in light of the fact that this patient never even scratched himself on the jagged pieces of glass as he burst through to his short-lived freedom. How he managed to escape without being mutilated is still a mystery to me as was much as anything that I saw during my brief stint. He was eventually rounded up at the local Women's Christian Temperance League information store front where he'd spent the day memorizing their literature then reciting it in a stentorian voice to terrified passers by. I managed to hang on for another week, but when I was in the process of admitting some clown who wanted nothing more than a little state-funded R&R and he took a swing at me while saying "Six-foot-two, eyes of blue, I'm going to kill you," I pulled the plug, punched the clock, loaded up the VW Squareback with my few belongings and drove straight through for 1,500 miles to Whitefish. Hey, I realize that eighty dollars a week is serious money, but enough is enough.

The place I'm standing in now smells like that hospital in Wisconsin. Antiseptic. Lifeless. And there is a pervading sense of desperation and fear running through the air. Not madness. Fear. It brings back memories I'm not interested in reliving. I don't like it here and am thinking about beating it back out the double doors when someone taps my shoulder. Startled, I turn and face a large, young man dressed all in white. What else? And he says "Follow me." I do and we began a labyrinthine journey across a desolate landscape consisting of acres and acres of white linoleum and stark white corridors that run to distant horizons, through countless locked doors and finally up a phone booth-sized elevator to the third floor. At least that's what the light on the control panel indicates. The door slides open. We march up to another front desk, the upper half encased in thick Plexiglas. My guide, who's said nothing during the trek, leans over and speaks through a vented hole in the enclosure. I can't hear what he says, but the nurse pushes a button on her phone, speaks briefly, then nods to the happy fellow. He turns to me and says "Wait here." He disappears through still another locked door down the high, lonesome terrain of a long, empty hallway.

A place like this makes me feel like I've lost my mind, that I'm not in here to talk with Sam as part of my job, but rather, I've been duped into coming here by well-meaning, though wildly obsequious people who I mistakenly believe are my friends. Devious souls who really want me out of their line of sight and committed for life, subjected to shock therapy, unspeakable institutional food stuffs and never-ending doses of lithium. I'm getting very nervous about this when I hear a voice boom out "You must be Ed Bouchee. I'm Dr. Moryn." I shook hands with a man who appears to be in his seventies. He has a strong grip and we play the tough guy game for a little bit. He's my height and approximate weight, about six-two and two-oh-five.

"I'm glad you made it. Sam's been saying your name off and on throughout the morning while working on his drawings. They're quite good and if he stays with it, he might get a book out of them."

I'd heard that one before.

"Can I talk with him now?"

"Most definitely. I'll take you to his room and the two of you can be alone for as long as you like, though an attendant will be outside the door," and he smiles the queerest smile I've ever seen. His lips curl up instantly. Then there are these huge white teeth flashing like warning beacons along a rocky sea coast, but the eyes remain the same, open but blank. He doesn't laugh. I'm starting to get the picture. The help is nuts and the patients or clients or whatever they're called these days are comparatively sane. Nothing has changed over the years in this respect. I follow Moryn as he opens the inevitable locked door and starts down a section of the hospital that is apparently a dormitory or repository, take your pick, for those people the state considers to be either a threat to themselves or the public at large or are hip to what's really going on in what most of us like to call "The Real World." When Moryn starts whistling the theme song to Rawhide, I know my assessment of the situation in here is right on the mark. I pray to my god for the strength to keep my wits about me and not make any mistakes. I really want to get out of here. All of the doors are locked right now. Moryn, between discordant bars of the tune, says that all of the clients have been secured prior to my arrival. Read "Locked away." I feel much better. At the end of the hall he stops in front of a white metal door, which he unlocks and pushes open. He stands looking in for a second, then enters. I hear him say "Sam? Ed Bouchee is here to talk with you. He drove all the way from Biederbeck over Pipestone Pass to be here." He motions me in with a wave of his hand. I look over my shoulder before doing so. My faithful guide is standing across the hall from me.

"Jesus! No wonder nobody ever gets better in these places," I mumble and walked in.

Sam is sitting at a small table by a window that is heavily reinforced with thick-gauge wire. This seems unnecessary. Who'd want to leap thirty feet to the ground below, but then I've never spent a night in this place, let alone a few years. Moryn smiles his flat-line smile and walks out the door leaving me alone standing behind Sam. For several minutes, maybe four or five hundred, he continues working on one of his bison pictures. Moryn's right. Sam is good. A small herd of the animals, about fifty, are gathered in a loose circle grazing, standing or lying down. The animals are on an isolated bench with steep cliffs cutting down along two sides. In the background is a severe range of mountains that roll, ridge after ridge, into the distance. A storm is working its way down on the herd. The country reminds me of The Rocky Mountain Front up near Glacier Park. Sam's work is detailed and accurate, but there is also a distinctive style to his drawing. This wasn't naturalistic naturalist-style work. There's a strong mood to the stuff, one of wildness and impending doom or something along those lines. I feel fear and oppression, the sensations working through me subtly but thoroughly. He works for a while longer, then puts his pencil down and examines the finished product.

"Actually it's Bison, Bouchee," he says with his back to me. I wait for him to say more, but he turns silent again. I notice more drawings on the bed. All good. Very good. Some show Indians brandishing spears while riding bareback as they run down fleeing buffalo. Others are studies of individual animals. Close-ups of heads, even a detail of the horns and another of a tail. Tails all over this story. Maybe Dirt is right. But one in particular catches my attention. It shows thirteen headless buffalo hanging from hooks that are suspended from a large tree limb that runs on out of the picture. That's all there is. No background or foreground. No tree trunk. Only the dead beasts and the limb. I count them to kill time. Thirteen. Odd number I think.

"Odd number to be sure, but the way it is, is the way it is," says Sam. I spin around. He's facing me. To say I'm spooked is a mild understatement. Mind-reading 101 here. There are dark half-circles under eyes that are red-rimmed, the iris's light blue. A pretty color. I realize that I was about to lose it. Commenting to myself on the color of the man's eyes. Get a grip, Bouchee. Sam smiles and motions for me to sit on the edge of the bed. I reach for a cigarette out of habit.

"Can't smoke in here, but can I have one?"

I shake two loose, hand him one and stick the other in my mouth. I reach over and flick the lighter for him. He draws deeply taking down a quarter of the thing in one drag. I light mine. We smoke without talking, just looking at each other. We flick our ashes on the floor. I'm feeling very nervous, weird.

"Relax. This place is crazy, but you'll be all right," he says. I wonder about all of the words he is now saying. I'd been told that he wasn't talking except for the bison thing. Maybe some mental dam broke the other day with Liz. Who knew? "I could always talk, but there is no one to trust. Not Liz. Not Mark. Not Moryn. Not him," and he jerks a thumb in the direction of the attendant standing stock-still twenty feet from us. "They'll know I can talk now. Doesn't matter. Bouchee, listen to what I have to say. Sure I'm crazy. Always will be from now on. I've seen too much that's horrible beyond words, more than I could handle. Nothing to do but ride the waves," and he laughs, an eerie, hopeless sound that echoes for an instant then dies away. "But what I will tell is real if you can read between the lines. You can do that can't you?"

"I'll do my best," I croak.

"Sure you will." He smiles at some inner joke and more than likely at my discomfort.

I hand him another smoke and the lighter. What damn difference does it make if he goes berserk and torches the room? Nothing much would burn. I'm sure that I'm never getting out of here, anyway. Sam looks at me as he snaps the lighter on and off, staring at the small flame. He holds the fire to the edge of his chair and I think "Here we go," but he flicks it off and tosses the thing to me.

"I don't think so," and a real smile flashes across his face for a moment. He knows what's going on, where he is and he also knows that he is unable to hold things together for more than a little while at a time. Whatever he's seen or experienced has done a serious number on him.

"Yes, that's true."

The way he has of commenting on everything I'm thinking, unnerves me. Telepathy, ESP and the rest of that New-Age jive annoys me. I don't buy any of it. All of it is a hustle practiced by predacious thieves to separate the hopelessly insecure from their money. Want to be an Indian. Give me twenty grand and you may call yourself He Who Roams The Sage. Want to talk to a ten-million-year-old medium to find out about your past. Give me fifteen grand and you can talk to Clarabell who's sitting next to me right here. God! Pathetic b.s. If I can get dressed and remember my name in the morning, I figure that I'm ahead of the game. What is going on in this room is just a series of coincidences. I hang on to that thought.

"I didn't kill Mark. He was my friend. What killed him is invisible to most of us," and he blows a cloud of smoke in my direction. "This is important. Hear what I say. Remember, between the lines. Mark was afraid of the dark. With good reason. The darkness is what killed him. My life has been dark for what seems like forever. So has yours and all of the rest of you. None of us are happy. We hide in the shadows. Afraid of the light. The darkness kills us all. It always has been that way. And it always will."

Seems like double-talk to me, but I'll think on it if I ever breathed free air again.

"And one more thing. Or is it two? Mark hated buffalo tails. Liz didn't," and he isn't smiling at all now. There is anger, make that pure rage shooting from his eyes. I can feel the heat of it. He holds my gaze for a long time, then turns around. He carefully places the completed drawing on the floor, pulls a clean sheet of thick paper from a stack beneath the table and starts in again. I wait for a long time to see if he will say anything else. He doesn't. Standing up, I leave the half-full pack of Camels on top of one of his drawings. As I'm passing through the door I hear him say.

"Actually it's bison."

The attendant locks Sam's door, moves ahead of me and unlocks the door at the end of the corridor. I pass through, one lock closer to freedom. Moryn is waiting near the elevator.

"We monitor his room and that's the most he's ever said to anyone, but it means nothing, I'm sure. I notice he went back to his catch line as you left. This happens all the time in situations like Sam's. They tire of the routine they have going for them and appear to come back to us, but they really don't. When someone new or unfamiliar visits, they either remain silent or on occasion do what Sam just did. For lack of a better way to put this, he was showing off," and the dear doctor shoots me his lurid smile.

The elevator door begins to open. I thank Moryn for his help, promising to keep him up to date on any new discoveries. He agrees to do the same and shakes my hand. The attendant pushes the G button on the panel and as the door slides shut, Moryn and his teeth disappear from view. In only minutes I am walking out into the warm air and sunshine. Lord! I'll let the bastards shoot me before they ever put me in there.

Sitting in the truck again, finally, feels like coming home after an eternal stay in some loony foreign country like Greece. I can't wait to see The Dog and then head up to Ray's for Happy Hour, to return to the real world, Biederbeck style. On the drive back I keep hearing the words "afraid of the dark," "buffalo tails," and "between the lines" as they repeat themselves in Sam's voice over and over, running through my head in bright white letters against a jet-black background. I wonder what Sam is trying to tell me, especially about Mark...and about Liz.

~~~

In his own way Miskis listens to people. He hears what they say. His survival and freedom depend on this. He rarely nods or gives any other indication that he agrees or disagrees with their thoughts or observations, but he listens. The other day in bed when Liz mentioned the potential trouble with the buffalo tails, the fact that a few people in Biederbeck are now talking about them and that one had been discovered by Bouchee at the murder scene, the comment registered in his mind. Normally he would not have given the matter any thought. So what if someone found something up there? He knows what he's doing, how to cover his tracks and how to make people see what he wants them to see in what is a form of instant hypnosis that he's perfected over the years. Really, in his mind it's more the power of suggestion that he slips into their heads while they are focused on the intense glare of his gaze. The mind hears what he wants planted but the conscious awareness of what he's doing is nonexistent. He learned this skill by examining how others used to be able to make him do things he had no interest in or disliked like cleaning up their messes, helping change a flat tire, small things like these. The few times these individuals succeeded with Miskis they'd maintained firm eye contact and spoke in even, soft tones. He refined this to make the process part of his every day routine, a part of his personality. He hardly ever thought about the actual mechanics of this anymore. He just worked his way on others when he needed something or wanted something accomplished.

When Liz said something she had a reason or premonition of things to come. Like the time she told him of her dream about a pair of fishermen who drowned while wading a small mountain stream. When a pair of Fish, Wildlife and Parks fisheries biologists found the bodies, they were tangled in a net caught on a bridge piling. So, instead of stringing his net the next day as he'd originally planned, he spent the day watching that stretch of Indian Creek from behind some trees. In the afternoon two flyfishers waded into view. They worked their way rapidly upstream, jumping from holding spot to holding spot only catching a few trout. If the net had been in place, the two would have discovered it. Liz's dream had saved him the trouble of killing the two and stashing the bodies far back in the hills.

In another vision she saw him encountering a younger woman at a bar in Coltrane and that this person could cause him trouble. Liz said she wasn't sure if the woman had brown or blonde hair, but that she was about five-feet-tall, tanned and athletically attractive. Later that week he stopped into that bar to get some cigarettes. Standing a short distance from him was a woman fitting the description so closely it made Miskis look twice. She had brown hair, but the last two inches had been bleached to the lighter color. On her shirt was the emblem of the U.S. Fish and Wildlife Service. He overheard her telling the bartender that she was on her way to the Park to work as part of the wolf recovery project.

He listened to Liz, all right. And she was always bringing him things from town that he needed, stuff he'd written down on a list in the morning and had never mentioned to her. Or she worked phrases that were running through his mind into her conversation, like one time when for no reason he could figure "I'll be there with bells on my toes" kept repeating itself in his head and she turned to him as she was leaving and said "I'll be back tomorrow with bells on my toes." She was always doing that, probably unconsciously, not that levels concerning their intimate forms of communication mattered. They'd grown far too close to even consider such trivialities. They were beyond what he considered the pedestrian aspects of ordinary man-woman connections. Because of all of this and much more he couldn't describe to himself, things that she showed him in unexplainable ways, he's learned to trust her instincts and act on what she tells him. Miskis is a predator and a survivor. He knows who is in the game at a high level and who is merely running a psycho-babble con.

As for the buffalo tails, he's held on to all of the things because in some curious way that even he can't understand, the tails are tangible symbols of his contempt for, as he sees things, the inherent weakness of the human race and the choice he made many years ago to turn away from what he considers a herd of sheep. All of them that is, except for Liz. But he doesn't consider her one of them. She's like him or more to the point, they've become the same person. He has no idea what love is. He's never even considered the question. His attraction to her is uncontrollable, without thought or conscious emotion. Being with her physically is intense. Everything in his life is intense. There's no room for moderation or holding back. Miskis is not made this way. Intense is the intrinsic way he feels things should be between them. When they are apart, when she is back in Coltrane or somewhere else, they are still one. He is always aware of her presence and the unique condition of what the two of them have become - an entity far beyond the basic sum of one plus one makes two. So, when she said what she did about the buffalo tails, he heard her and acted on her concern.

There are over one-hundred of the cropped tails that he keeps in cedar Monte Cruz double corona cigar boxes stored in an old steamer trunk that he found in the shed when he bought the place. He gathered them up and placed them carefully on the floor of his truck. He'd considered burning them in the wood stove, but the thought of the stench as they flared into flame and were reduced to ashes seemed wrong, a bad idea. He'd risked a lot to kill, butcher and sell the end products of these animals that were no longer a part of the Siksika's sacred herd. He laughed at the irony of all of this, especially the fact that white men are the ones doing the killing of the buffalo and sticking it to the Indians one more time. History always repeats itself. That's clear to him after reading dozens of books on the early years of the white man in the America West. He'd often thought of how the whites had tamed this tribe giving them a reservation that stretched from the eastern base of the northern Rockies all the way to the North Dakota border. As cattle grew in importance and ranchers recognized the value of the land's protein-rich grasses, as gold, silver, oil and gas were discovered, the reservation shrank until today it's about the size of Glacier National Park. 'A little piece of not a hell of a lot,' he said to Grace once. And now he is doing more of the same to these people in a way that may seem minor to those on the outside, but in fact rips at the tribe in fundamental spiritual and cultural ways. If he is ever caught by members of the tribe they'd killed him after torturing him in some remote canyon or on top of a windy butte. If any of the authorities arrest him for this, he'll be in the state prison at Deer Lodge doing hard time. Freedom is everything to Miskis. More valuable than gold or diamonds. He knows he'll be dead within a day, two at most, inside of that place, or any place that holds him against his will. They'll have to kill him first. This is all he considers. He risks all of this because money is freedom and to place his ability to move throughout the world whenever he wants in his own way appeals to the contrary nature of a small, but powerful, facet of his personality, one he once tried to fight or change, but realized was impossible to resist. Being pragmatic, he accepted this weakness years ago and raised his level of meticulous planning and ruthless caution another notch. He logically decides to bury these totems that mark his dark, violent life and eliminate their potential threat in the process.

He is not like the Siksikas who respect and revere all animals and their spirits - like the buffalo which once gave them life; or the grizzly, that the Indians fear, avoid and regard as a sacred animal of great supernatural as well as physical power; or the golden eagle whose feathers decorate Siksika war bonnets and shields, a bird that can only be captured by brave members of the tribe who claim to possess a vast and secret power. None of this means anything to Miskis.

He decides to drive up the two-track behind his cabin to an old-growth stand of Ponderosa he discovered one fall. In the middle of the pines stands one tree that is much larger and older than all the others. This pine is several feet thick at the base. One massive, gnarled limb reaches out from the trunk for nearly forty feet, more than a third as long as the tree is tall. The Ponderosa is hundreds of years old, surviving the fierce weather that has swept down from the mountains for centuries before whites ever visited this country. That tree was growing while herds of bison many miles long and deep thundered across the prairies. And the Ponderosa grew during the decades of white men coming first as explorers, then trappers and traders along with the military, and then cattle barons miners and homesteaders. The tree lived through all of this and possibly more to come. He'll dig a deep hole and bury the tails here. That makes sense to him. Better than casually tossing the things in the fire.

He isn't interested in the spiritual aspects of animals or their mythology. His is a much more straight-forward existence. A dark one, but in a way, one ruled by logic, dominated by survival. This holds true even with Liz. How they are together now, their closeness, is something necessary that's happened for a reason. He knows that.

The awareness is sufficient. He doesn't care about the how and why of life. He only lives to roam and do what he does. He accepts without a trace of thought the things that come his way. He unconsciously assimilates them into his life. There is no romance or willingness to give completely of himself or share his life with her. These things naturally happen in a predefined order. She is necessary to his existence. That's all. He's never considered what life would be without her. That isn't in his nature. He moves through the moments as they present themselves in their relentless succession without any consideration for the past or future or the consequences his actions on others or even on himself may have. He literally exists. That is all. Still, something tells him that he should bury the stubs beneath this one old pine tree. Again, he won't examine why he should do this. He just knows that he should.

After a long drive back to the timbered base of the mountains he comes to a large grassy meadow filled with small groups of whitetails. They drift into the trees when he drives by. He crosses this and reaches the stand of Ponderosa. A flock of pine siskuns calling among themselves lends a background hum to the setting. Stellar Jays intrude on the chorus with their rowdy calls. As he unloads the boxes he hears the wail of a wolf riding the waves of cool air sweeping down from above. Definitely a wolf. He's familiar with this cry, has heard it sailing over the North Fork of the Flathead River and even in the timbered mountains of the upper Yaak River drainage years ago before fly fishing guides, developers and hack writers had plundered that fine country. The sound is unmistakable, and nothing like the chattering bark and laughter of a coyote. This is the wail of a fierce, powerful beast. One howl, then all is silent. He carries the tails to the tree and goes back for a pick and shovel. He hears the long, moaning call again, much closer this time, less than a mile. Despite all the pretentious science of the biologists in Yellowstone Park coupled with the dogma uttered by countless uninformed animal lovers, every resident in the region knows that wolves are running free in the Yellowstone and most everywhere else up this way. They've been doing so for years. Hearing one in the Nortons, less than one-hundred miles from the Park, seems completely natural to Miskis. Why wouldn't a lone animal or even pack be in these mountains? There's plenty of deer to eat. Few humans make this range their home. The land is wild, unspoiled and relatively isolated. There's good water, thick forest and open grassy benches – ideal wolf habitat.

He hammers away at the rocky ground, the tip of the pick chipping rocks as he digs deeper. Every so often he drops this tool and grabs the shovel to clear out the soil he's loosened. When the hole is nearly five-feet-deep he stops digging, climbs out and lights a Bolivar Royal Corona cigar. He draws down on it, then blows the smoke across the tip making it glow orange-red. As he does this he hears the wolf again. The animal sounds like it is on the ridge behind him less than a quarter-mile away. He tosses the burning cigar in the hole forgetting the fact that the Siksika consider tobacco an offering to their gods, one they make when they are asking for food or strength and purity of thought to experience visions that will guide them in the future. He puts the boxes with the buffalo tails in the ground. Then he back fills the hole, tamps down the dirt as much as possible and finishes the job by scattering needles, pine cones and dry grass over the digging.

Back at the truck as he opens the door he looks up. He senses a presence nearby. The wolf is staring at him. The large animal is standing on the ground where the tails are buried. The wolf's fur is dark gray mixed with coal-black and patches of tan, the tail long and bushy. It looks exactly like the wolves he's seen ghosting along Rock Creek drainage in the Yukon a few miles north of the Arctic Circle. He'd been up that distant way on an exploratory trip for possible game poaching operations he'd only just begun a dozen years ago. Great land, but rough and too far from any reasonable distribution point, so he stayed with Montana. The wolf never moves. It stands and watches him with dark eyes that show with hot yellow-white circles in their centers. Miskis returns the gaze. The two are looking at each other, not the same species to be sure, but the same kind of being all the same. Predators. He reaches for the rifle hanging on the rack in the cab and brings it slowly to him. He raises the gun to firing position and takes aim on the animal's left eye. The creature remains motionless. Miskis pulls the trigger. The wolf drops to the ground dead on top of the grave for the bison tails. The harsh sound of the shot dies quickly on the still air. The gunsmoke lingers.

Miskis replaces the rifle, gets in the truck and drives back to the cabin.

~ ~ ~

"Count, October Fest is still more than two months off. Don't you think you're rushing things a bit?" This is directed at the tall, heavy-set figure looming over my desk. He's dressed in Bavarian attire complete with brown lederhosen held up by suspenders that have a pattern of weight lifters standing on each other's shoulders, one on top of another, beige knee socks, white shirt, and dark green coat with a matching vest. A sporty hat featuring a clump of some kind of animal fur jutting out from the band complete the tasteful ensemble. Knowing the Count, the fur was probably plucked from a road-killed badger or worse. An enormous ceramic beer mug is clutched in his right hand. Count Campau stands out as an eccentric in a town full of eccentrics. The outfits he wears are, shall we say, creative. Thankfully he doesn't recognize Halloween because he fears calling up any more evil spirits than "are already lurking in the back alleys of our fair town." Thanksgiving, Christmas, St. Patrick's Day, Valentine's Day, Easter and July 4th, among others, are all fair game, receiving his determined attention. His getups for Veteran's Day are over the top. Last year he appeared as WWII British General Montgomery. I know, doesn't sound like much, but the Count is six-five and two-hundred-twenty pounds. Monty was more in the neighborhood of five-eight, one-forty. No one knows for sure what the Count does for a living. Some say he repairs major appliances. He's always been able to jump start my refrigerator when ever it collapses like some overweight stock broker in the midst of a full-blown heart attack following the news that the FTC is investigating his incessant and unnecessary back-and-forth stock transactions that do nothing more than accrue large sales fees for the broker. Others think that he might be selling vinyl siding and aluminum gutters over in Birney. Anything's possible. He's out of town often enough and he has a flair for the kind of nonsensical yet appealing conversation that's the bread-and-butter of pitchmen everywhere.

"Never too early, Bouchee. Never too early. But that's not why I'm here anyway." The Count seemed to be moving in the direction of apoplexy. His face is crimson shading to purple. "Dirt just told me about the buffalo tail you found. Actually it's bison," and I think 'Damn. Here we go again.' The Count strides over to the refrigerator and grabs a beer, my last bottle of Whitefish Brewery's Pale Nut Brown Ale. Popping the cap off with his thumb, he demolishes the sixteen-ounce beverage or bevy as he likes to call them, in seconds, brown foam running down his chin and splatting on the floor. He then turns his attentions to his mug and drains that baby in one take. I'm expecting an enormous, window-rattling burp, but the Count cuts me a break and behaves himself. The Dog pretends to ignore him, but watches his every move with one partially-open eye. Ever since the Count had accidentally dropped a twenty-eight-pound turkey on him at a holiday brunch two winters ago, The Dog is extremely wary. "I know a little something about those tails or maybe something related to them. A friend of mine with the Siksika tribe told me last week when I was up there fishing Beargrass Lake ... took four rainbows over ten pounds and lost two others even larger. Using Gray Ghosts and Hornbergs. Should have seen the ..."

"Count, try and keep it on the road here, please."

"Oh ... sorry about that ... fishing gets my blood

working you know."

"I noticed."

"Well, we found a couple of buffalo stones in the dried mud while poking around with ski poles along the shore. They're little fossilized dinosaurs and one thing led to another and I asked my friend how his herd was doing and he said not well at all," and the Count snatches my last bottle of Anchor Steam Ale. I'm starting to take a serious hit here. I pass on asking what they were doing with ski poles while out fly fishing. They're only so many hours in a day. The Dog has had enough and gets up with a grunt, disappearing into a hallway closet. He often spends hours in there and I never ask him what goes on in the darkness. We all need our private moments. "He mentioned that their herd was not any bigger, perhaps smaller, than when they'd started a few years back as you may remember. No one can figure out why. Seemed quite put out by the whole affair. Can't say that I blame him in the least when I ponder the matter. They've had a rough go of it since we whites forced ourselves on them. Nobody among his people, handsome creatures every one of them by the by, has an answer. Especially no one on the council. A big mystery, I'd say. So when Dirt told me about your finding a buffalo tail. Actually it's ..."

"Count. Please."

"Sorry. Can't help myself sometimes. Words seem to come out of nowhere, words that must be spoken my good fellow. At any rate, when I heard this, a light went on in my head." From what I'd seen over the years, it must look like a night game at the original Comiskey Park inside of there. "Maybe that tail came from one of the Siksika's

156

vanishing buffalo. Vanishing buffalo. Not bad if I ...

"Count! Show a little mercy here. I'm not what I used to be," and I get up a retrieve a Mike's Hard Lemonade from the fridge. Horrible stuff, but tough times call for tough action. The cap is locked on tight. I cut my hand on it while twisting it off, and then take a long drink. Horrible. Some days are like this.

"Most inconsiderate on my part. I'll come to the point. Maybe some well-monied sports from out-of-state, Delaware or Texas, somewhere obscure like that, are running up there and popping one or two when no one is looking. Some of these so-called hunters just like to kill things for the sake of killing. A staged hunt, if you will, designed so that the pathetic wretches can brag to their cronies about the wild beasts they've dropped from 500 hundred yards at a full gallop and have the head mount to back up the specious claims. Bovine slaughter to my way of looking at the odious situation. Maybe. Maybe not, but I just had to tell you what I was thinking. Hope you don't mind the intrusion?"

"Not at all," but the Count is already out the door talking about getting someone named Danny O'Keefe to perform for the Fest. The Count's a piece of work. I replay the conversation in my head, but nothing really strikes a chord. I mean after talking with Sam and Dirt I am beginning to seriously consider the possibility that the tail I'd found is connected in some oddly oblique way with Grace's murder, but the connection with the Siksika's herd seems too far out there. Their reservation is over two-hundred miles away from the Norton's. To believe the tail came from that group of animals seems to be quite a stretch. Still, this whole deal is not ordinary, more like twisted and frightening. The phone's ringing interrupts my thoughts.

~ ~ ~

"I'm so glad you could come out this afternoon. The loneliness is awful. And I really needed to talk with you about Sam and all that's going on," Liz says as she hands me a glass of lemonade. "I think you'll enjoy this." She watched as I took a sip. Not bad. In fact, damn good. Not up to Mike's lofty standards, but still tasty. Probably due to the healthy addition of George W. Dickel's, judging from the amber tint and the bite. We are sitting in the sun on the front porch of her and Sam's home which is located on a rise a few miles outside of Coltrane. They have a nice place here. A fair-sized cottage with a small creek flowing down a narrow crease in the land not far from the front of the house. The sides of the structure are covered with wisteria, the dark green leaves lending a peaceful green shade to the place. The grass has been allowed to grow wild, a couple of feet high with wildflowers sprinkled around. The view is pretty good, too. The wide, open valley gives way to mountain peaks everywhere - the Nortons, Buffalos and the Weirs, all of them shimmer in the distance. Liz looks good herself. Tanned. Cutoffs and bikini top. More relaxed than I've ever seen her. A sense of calmness appears to have settled over her. I know she's married and I like and want to help both her and Sam, but I can't help but noticing what an attractive women she is. I work at turning my thoughts in a more appropriate, professional direction with modest success. I examine the possibility of talking about the work I was doing for her.

Seems like a good idea.

"Strong enough for you?"

"Yes. Haven't had one of these since college. Not a bad change of pace from straight bourbon. It's similar to switching back and forth between Camels and Newports. The menthol clears the throat and then the straights taste good again, but I really need to quit," I said while lighting a smoke.

"Seems a shame to give it up now that it sounds like you have things lined out with the tobacco. It really is so rare when an individual actually fine-tunes a bad habit and bad habits are the best kind. The ones that can kill you always seem to have the most to offer, even if they finish us off in the end," and she laughs while freshening my glass of lemonade. "I wonder why that is, that the dangerous aspects of living are the most intriguing and seductive. Perhaps that are those among us, present company excepted, of course, who prefer living on the edge, playing games with death even though they know full well that death always wins sooner or later. Maybe some of us just can't accept life when things are going smoothly and well. I've wondered about this many times, especially since Mark's murder. But back to my original point. I'd hate to see you quit. You're doing so well with those things."

We both laugh. Nothing like bad habits to bring out the humor in people.

I look over at her. I smell the perfume she is wearing, and I say to myself 'Bouchee, you're a dead man.' And another voice inside said 'So what if she is married.' I doubted that Sam was ever going to see the light of day again. He's parked in Turbid Springs for, from all I can tell, the rest of his life. He's long gone, and lyrics from the Zappa album "Freakout," the ones about someone named Suzy Creamcheese and her meanderings in Kansas, bounce around in my head. I fail to see the connection, but my mind often has a mind of its own and isn't it funny how we overlook some great music for a while, say twenty-five years. That's truly hysterical and I realize that I'm mentally treading water, trying desperately to avoid the truth of the matter here, the one that says that I'm becoming hopelessly hooked on Liz despite my friendship with Sam and my complete awareness that all of what I'm feeling is dead wrong and is going to no doubt lead to a lot of trouble and hardship. I really must get a grip here. But I realize that aside from Dirt, I've never seen her talk at length with anyone else around town. Not at Ray's or The Night Hawk or in any other place. And I enjoy talking with her, spending time with this woman. Other than Sam, there is no one else that she's interested in that I'm aware of. All I pray for his patience for all of this lunacy to work itself out, and hopefully in a way where none of us gets hurt or that this murder grows any more complicated than it already is. Hope and pray, I've done a lot of this over the years with mixed results. Either Liz is playing the part of the good wife or no one's gotten her attention so far or both. Humans being humans, who the hell knows why we do some of the crazy things we do. No doubt I'm that man, someone who's happened along at the right time. Right. Nearly fifty. Banged-up by hard living, with tons of money in the bank. Plenty to offer this unique person. A man who is capable of granting her every wish and who can make her dreams come true, even ones that she hasn't imagined yet. There is no doubt about it, I must be the one. I try once again to put this silly line of reasoning away in some distant corner of my mind, at least for now, but she leans over to get a cigarette from the pack on the low table between us. She puts the thing between her lips and edges ever closer to me, smiling some more, eyes twinkling and full of mischief. I strike a match for her. She holds my gaze as she eases very slowly and confidently back into her chair and languidly stretches out her shapely, brown legs that reach all the way to big-time trouble and back. I know now that what few redeeming morals and social values I desperately cling to have just sailed off out of sight on the day's western breeze. Life is too short and her legs are too long for me to do what most people like to think is the right thing in this situation. Take the high road and stick to business. No chance of that. I want to spend more time with Liz, a lot more. I want to hold her right now.

"Anything you'd like to say or have to tell me ... about anything."

I almost say what I really had wanted to, but hang on as best I can in a last futile attempt at responsibility and decorum. Instead, I compliment her on the perfume.

"It's called First. The only one I like the scent of. The rest are too sweet or way too strong." She blushes at this. "Anyway, this is the last of it."

"I'll buy you some next time I'm in Billings," and now I know for sure that I am through, over the edge crazy about her. Offering to buy a woman perfume? I've never done that in my life.

"Oh, don't even consider it," she says. "It costs over

one-hundred dollars an ounce or something like that."

"I'll sell The Dog."

At this she laughs uncontrollably. The remark doesn't seem that funny. I wonder if I'm serious. No I don't. The Dog's my friend, a loyal companion. They're aren't too many of those wandering around these days. A good woman is worth everything. The loyalty of my dog is worth more. Even in my extremely excited state I realize this much.

"What's the joke," I ask.

"You'd never understand. I'm not sure that I do. You just make me laugh sometimes. Thank you."

I decide to push on by recounting my visit with Sam, replaying our conversation word-for-word, a skill, if you can call it that, I'd learned while working for a small daily newspaper several lifetimes ago. I interviewed high school coaches, who on a good day with a strong tail wind, exhibited flat-line self-absorption or I talked with the terminally venal so I could pad advertising puff pieces disguised as in-depth features on health clubs or car washes. After doing this for a week or two, I acquired this ability out of some misplaced need to remain marginally sane. The individuals I interviewed, and I use this term loosely, would hold forth for decades and I'd move my pen across a notepad never scrawling an intelligible word, playing the part of a hot-shot reporter, which I wasn't. I didn't have the ability to get the story and write it down without my rampant personal feelings and opinions getting in the way. I admire individuals who can do this, but I'm not one of them. When asked, I explained away the scribbling as my own form of short-hand. While all of this verbiage was spewing forth, my mind would be miles away fishing small mountain creeks or I'd imagine myself killing the paper's managing editor in the perfect murder. I took my sanity seriously in those days.

Liz is quiet for awhile after I'd finish my report. This time I freshened our drinks from the pitcher. I take a long sip and watch a pair of red-tail hawks working along the hill across the creek. The birds soar in slow circles at the same altitude and about a quarter-mile apart. They glide easily down the ridge on the breeze. Soon they are too far away for me them see anymore, at first fading into tiny dots, then there is nothing. The birds are gone over a distant rise.

"Moryn is probably right. I think Sam is bored. And Sam's right about one thing, too," she says. "He'll never come out of the darkness. Not ever again. He's always been in and out of that place since I've known him, but the last two years he's stayed there more and more. Each time there's a little less Sam when he comes back to me. It's like I don't know who he is now and the love we had has changed and weakened. I feel more and more alone with each episode. It's like I'm married to a phantom or even less. I don't have a very clear idea what happened before I knew him to make him the way he is. Whenever I try to get him to talk about his moods, he gets mad and says they aren't moods, that life is the way it is, filled with more pain than anything else. I even suggested that we sell off some of our stocks, enough to move some place out of this world, say Chile or even Dawson Creek up in British Columbia, but he always shakes his head and says no way, that they, whoever they are, will bury him in Montana.

That I don't understand, so I finally gave up. He's stuck in this continual 'Poor me. Nothing can be done to improve things' loop. I'm tired of the attitude, the loneliness and the futility of all of it."

I start to say something about medication possibly smoothing out these mood swings and to ask about their stocks, an asset that I was unaware of, but she went on "And, like I said before, there's nothing to the buffalo tails. Absolutely nothing. I'm sure of it. I've been thinking about the tail and it just leads me nowhere, like so many things in my life that look important and amount to nothing. Sam sees something in the woods or even on TV, then works it around in his head until it takes on real or surreal proportions. He gets to the point where imagination becomes reality after thinking about it, working it around in his mind, a million times."

And then I jump in and tell her what the Count told me that morning. She throws back her head and howls. She laughs for a long time. The tears running down her cheeks, and unlike that first visit in my office, this time they are from the appreciation of a rich joke.

"Everyone in that town is off-the-wall. You know that and you're no better than the rest of them from what little I've seen. You and that goofy dog. Who cares. It's all a joke anyway. The harder we try, the more we screw up and the funnier things become. Don't you agree? And the Count. I saw Campau a couple of days ago wandering around town dressed like a refugee from The Black Forest, talking away to himself. Something about someone named Good Time Charlie who had the blues and another one named O'Keefe. Like either of those characters exist anywhere but in The Count's imagination. How he stays on the loose, I'll never know."

"I've wondered that myself a few times." We both laugh and look at each other. She is beautiful. I really am a dead man. "As for his outfit, he's all fired up about October Fest. Doesn't take much to set him off ... and I don't mean to be stubborn, but something about that damn buffalo tail keeps pulling at me. I have no idea what it is, but it's something, that's all I can say. I really would like to stay with this for awhile longer."

"Forget about it, for my sake. Let's be friends and drop the rest of it. I'm trying as hard as I can to push through all of the hell and accept the fact that my husband has been a seriously troubled soul for a very long time. Maybe all his life and that he'll probably never get any better. That horrible murder was the finishing touch. It almost was for me."

She reaches for another cigarette. It's all I could do to keep from reaching for her.

"Every time I go over all of this I try to find something, any little thing, that will let me hang on to the idea that Sam is innocent. The more I do, the more I see that he most likely killed Mark, that all of the drinking finally pushed him too far. He's the only man I've ever really loved in my life and I don't want to let go of him, but I have to," and the smile this time was not a happy one. "As selfish as this sounds, to let go for my own sake, I must do it. All of this is tearing me up and wearing me down. I want to move on with life. Qualls had it right from the start and I'm trying to accept that.

"I can talk with you. I'm so tired of all of the others.

Ignorant people I can understand. Stupid people I can tolerate for awhile, but idiots, the one's who refuse to hear a word that I say ... spending five minutes talking with them is like having little pieces of my mind sliced off like chunks from a wedge of cheese. The whole race is becoming nothing but a bunch of inbred imbeciles." She looks at me with a sad expression and says "I'm sorry. I get carried away and feel sorry for it all sometimes, especially myself and that's disgusting. Forgive me."

She stands up and walks to the railing. I hear her start to cry. I walk over and put my hands on her shoulders. The skin feels smooth and warm. We stay like this for a long time. Then she turns around in my arms and she's not crying anymore. She wraps her arms around me. We kiss. As simple as that. We kiss.

"I enjoy you. You're not like what Sam's become at all. You laugh at things and you're not all that hard to figure out."

She pushes her body hard against mine and all of a sudden we're lying in the sun making love, unrestrained, wildly. Spontaneous is the only word for it. I feel like I've been with her for years. I hear myself say "I love you, Liz," and think to myself while saying this 'You're a complete loser, buddy,' but that passes in an instant.

~ ~ ~

Liz didn't sleep around. That wasn't her style or part of how she conducted her life. In twelve years of marriage she'd been unfaithful just one time, with a nine-ball pool hustler she'd gotten to know while doing a story for Billiard's Digest. She loved pool, knew the magazine's editor and when she learned the player was coming to town for an exhibition at The Round The Bend bar, she nailed down the assignment. The two of them were attracted to each other at first sight. This was one time where one thing really did lead to another. When the tryst was over, she never saw the man again. Liz felt bad for Sam about her infidelity. She never told him and went out of her way to be attentive and affectionate from there on out. That was the only time. Very few men interested her. She often thought that they behaved like ego-crazed children. She'd much rather suffer through the increasingly frequent hard times with Sam than endure the secrecy, lies and disappointments she associated with her lone affair. Once was enough in that terribly lonely arena. The guilt she carries with her from the incident gnaws at her stomach with the low-grade pain of anxiety.

When Bouchee told her about finding the stub of buffalo tail at Indian Creek she immediately realized she'd made a mistake hiring him. Her plan had been to engage his services in order to try and divert attention from both her and husband. Something along the lines of an obvious misdirection. So obvious that no one would think that the behavior was anything other than what she intended them to think it was. A wife desperately trying to clear her husband who she loved deeply, which she was and did. She wanted everyone to believe that she was doing everything in her power to find the real murderer. Weirdly enough, this is exactly how she felt. Miskis had such a strong and even perverse hold on her that Liz was having a difficult time knowing how she felt about Sam, Bouchee or herself. There were times, times that were becoming more and more common, where she wasn't sure what was going on, what was really true or who she really was. Each day life grew more confusing and disorienting for her. The only time she felt like she wasn't losing her mind was when she was with Miskis, though she realized, at least vaguely, that this was because the man controlled her, directed her and manipulated her thinking in calculating ways that created the illusion of direction and normalcy.

Unfortunately and to her surprise Bouchee is proving to be more determined and intuitive than is good for her and Miskis, who expressed strong doubts about employing the strategy and the detective to begin with. He felt that introducing any variables into an equation that contained a logical and satisfactory outcome as it stood initially was a mistake. From what she'd seen of him around Biederbeck, she assumed he was just one more hard-drinking, well-meaning, middle-aged guy. The fact that he is also a writer added to this impression. She'd had plenty of experience with the writing game over the years. Liz learned long ago that there is no glamour to writing and no money to speak of unless you pimped yourself and wrote self-serving, disingenuous garbage or got lucky. She gave Bouchee credit for playing it straight with this work. His articles never pulled any punches. They were hard and tough. His one novel based on a proposed mine west of the mountains was good. Damn good she thought. Dirt told her the sales of that book did not even cover the three-thousand dollar advance. She laughed cynically at this and told Dirt that maybe Bouchee should write books about vampires or nuclear war or fabricated returns of non-existent wolf packs to some isolated northwest Montana mountain range if fame and fortune were the objects of his efforts. Dirt said simply 'Bouchee writes because he has to. He could care less about the rest of that stuff.' Liz knew then that Dirt respected the guy, a rare thing coming from him. Just about everyone in town wanted Dirt's attention. He commanded respect. His national reputation as an artist could be a real asset to a mid-list, struggling writer. The right word from Dirt in the right ear could turn a book into a good selling proposition, so he was continually hit up for book blurbs and phone numbers of influential friends. He rarely complied and didn't give a damn what the petitioners thought of his uncooperative stance. Dirt added that Bouchee never asked him for help and once vehemently refused Dirt's offer to blurb the mining novel saying 'If the book has legs, it will stand on its own.'

And Liz was worried about that goofy but loveable dog of Bouchee's. He's the one who that found the tail to begin with. 'God, trouble seems to show up from the strangest places,' she said to Miskis recently. She laughed some at this, realizing that trouble appears when it wants from wherever it wants like a bad news in-law during the holidays. Now because of Bouchee and his dog, people in town know more than they should. People like Dirt Tidrow and that crazy but intuitive Count. The tail could lead the police right to Mark's killers. She decided that she had to do something. The easiest way she knows of gaining a man's attention and controlling him is with her body. This has always worked for her and other women she knows in the past, except with Miskis, but what is growing between them is uncommon, extraordinary.

There are no wants or expectations where he is concerned. Their relationship is completely different from anything she's experienced in the past. As for Bouchee, this little romance with him will continue for as long as it takes. She really likes the guy, more so each day. If she didn't like him she wouldn't be able to go on with this cruel charade. She doesn't want to hurt him, but she's in too deep now and Miskis has totally convinced her to follow through with her original plan. That it's either hurt Bouchee or run the huge risk of exposing themselves and their actions to the police. She tells him that she'll keep on with Bouchee until he and everyone else forgets all about the case. The deception, the dishonesty, is the price Liz believes that she must pay to maintain their freedom. She doesn't want to cause pain to this man that she's lying with right now, but she knows that she must. Her mind is with Miskis, even now. He is aware of her at this moment on some level. She can feel his presence within her and can see his face when she closes her eyes.. Liz isn't making love to Bouchee, she's making love to Miskis. He and who they are together is all that matters. Not anyone else, not herself as an individual only what the two of them have become together.

~ ~ ~

Back by the mountains beneath the ancient Ponderosa the wolf's lifeless body is cooling on the pine needles. The wind has died down and the forest is silent. A grizzly approaches, moving cautiously out from the protection of a thick cluster of aspens nearby. The large animal, more than a thousand pounds and covered with a thick coat of brown fur tipped with gray, swings its head from side to side tasting the air with its nose. The scent of the recently departed man is strong, as is the acrid smell of gunpowder and the truck's exhaust, scents that the bear has learned to fear. And there is something else, something unfamiliar. He turns in the direction of the slain wolf. The bear moves to the body where it rests on its side, the animal's one remaining eye glazed over, its thick tongue extended between rows of jagged teeth. The grizzly sniffs the animal and backs away. Then it rises on its hand legs and extends its fore paws. The bear remains standing this way, motionless, for a long time. The sun's dying light slices through the trees illuminating the two creatures in a golden glow.

In time darkness moves in.

-THREE-

THE LEAVES ON THE COTTONWOODS ARE STARTING TO TURN from dark green to yellow. In another week they will be blazing away shining like the October sun against a deep blue sky. Up this far, Indian Creek is less than thirty feet wide and averaging not more than a couple of feet deep, but the stream has its secrets, too. The rush of spring runoff over the seasons has carved deep, undercut banks and swift, deep channels that glide strongly along brushy overhangs. Large trout live here, hidden in shadowy safety, in protected solitude where they can rush out and smash smaller fish or gulp stray grasshoppers. Brown trout are beginning to stack up along these runs by the hundreds. Fish are digging redds next to undercut banks, below the tail-outs of pools and out in the middle of the stream in shallow riffles. The trout turn on their sides and push their tails back and forth flushing silt that has accumulated since last fall, the debris washing downstream in ever-thinning clouds. This motion also creates shallow depressions in the streambed gravels. The spawning areas are easy to see. Oval patches of light stone stand out from the dusky copper rocks that the trout have left alone. The redds are everywhere. Dozens and dozens in this quarter-mile length of water. Browns finished with their work hold just below the beds, riding easily in softer current. Some of the males weigh six or seven pounds. The shift into their breeding phase has produced dramatic changes. The males display long, curved lower jaws or kypes. Humps have formed on their backs. The color of the fish is intensified, glowing now in rich yellows and browns shading to almost black along the dorsal. The fins shine with the color of rich clover honey. Black spots run along their bodies and flecked tails worn ragged from the digging. Mixed in with all of these are blood-red spots highlighted by aureoles of soft silver. The browns are adorned in full spawning color. Wild, spectacular fish.

Miskis notices none of this as he drags one end of the gill net across the creek. The other end is now firmly lashed to the aspen he'd picked out a few weeks ago. He climbs up through a clump of alders and pushes through the thick undergrowth to a cottonwood on the opposite bank. He secures the ropes around the tree, cinching them down as tight as possible. The net stretches across the stream, not quite taught, but tight enough. He walks back to the bank and takes some time to examine the water. He sees the males holding where they are. They're hard to miss. He notices a few smaller females circling the redds, occasionally gliding over them, and even drifting down to their mates, the pairs holding together in the slower water. He hadn't expected so many fish after all that he and Grace killed off the past few seasons. And spawning is early this year. The hot, dry weather has changed the pattern, moved things up a week or two. A pleasant surprise that means more money and sooner than expected. Splashing nearby attracts his attention. Two males are already impaled by their gills in the net. The more they thrash, the more enmeshed they became. Blood runs down their sides and splatters on their gill covers. Miskis decides that he'd better check the net in the morning. There will be a lot of dead and dying brown trout to deal with. The next few days will be busy ones.

~ ~ ~

I've been seeing Liz for several weeks both in an investigative capacity and as someone who is very much interested in her as a woman. We've grown close, spending the time up at her place taking walks, talking or merely sitting out on the deck in the sun quietly enjoying each other's company. I've never met a woman like her before. She's perceptive, giving and genuinely interested in my life. The first woman I've known with all of these qualities. When we aren't up by Coltrane, we're back in town hanging out at The Night Hawk or at Round The Bend or over having drinks and dinner at Ray's. Dirt thinks that I'm in over my head, but also has expressed his doubts about both Liz's taste and mental stability.

"I mean Bouchee, how sane can she really be if she's indeed actually interested in you," he said one night while she was on the phone in the lobby. "No offense, but I have a hard time figuring it all. Enjoy the good times while they last, because it often seems like they never have a long run for guys like us."

Typical Dirt, but I heard him and intend to take his advice.

Some afternoons we'd drive out onto the high plains west of town with The Dog and go hunting for sharp-tails and Huns. We'd walk behind The Dog as he thoroughly searched the covers scaring up dozens of birds. He'd never worked better or closer. I could tell that Liz loved him. Each time he returned with a bird she would praise him and remove clumps of burrs tangled in the curly hair of his ears with a heavy duty metal comb she's purchased for the task. By the end of the second day with the three of us hunting together The Dog would drop the birds at her feet instead of at mine. He was particularly proud of the retrieve he made on a lone sage grouse I shot. The large bird popped up out of a tangle of grass and sage and beat it down wind in a flurry of buff, yellow and gray feathers, clucking all the way. I dropped it about forty yards out and Liz shouted "Great shot," and gave me a smile that buckled my knees. The Dog snorted and huffed his way around and through the cover where the bird had fallen, pushed into the stuff, disappearing from view for a long time. Then he squirted out and came prancing back with the bird in his mouth, head held high and tail wagging. He placed the grouse at her feet and she dropped to her knees cooing "Good boy. That's a good boy. What a handsome dog." It was clear to see that she cared for him. I was beginning to believe that The Dog thought Liz was his long-lost mother. The weather had been flat-out gorgeous this fall. The time we spent together had been even better.

I now realize that I can devote the rest of my life to this woman and she's mentioned once or twice that she's going to divorce Sam not too far in the future. He isn't getting any better. He's eating next to nothing now. Liz said he is pale, gaunt and looks almost as bad as when she found him up at Indian Creek. He's stopped drawing buffalo or even speaking. Not even an "Actually it's bison" anymore. He hasn't said a word in two weeks.

The buffalo tail proved to be a dead end. I checked everywhere, with Fish and Game, the U.S. Fish and Wildlife Service, the university in Bozeman, the manager of Ted Turner's herd over in the Gallatin Valley, everywhere. Nothing turned up. Absolutely nothing. Even Dirt's stopped talking about the thing, concentrating his attentions instead on the chances of the Cubs losing one-hundred games this season. They were picked in the preseason to win their division, but then the Cubs are the Cubs. Currently the hapless team is sixty-and-ninety-five with one week to go. Dirt said with a good deal of excitement last night that they only had to go two-and-five the rest of the way to reach the century mark. There's no way the Cubs are ever going to reach the Series in our lifetimes, so Dirt explained that if you're going to be a loser, be a world-class one. Losing a hundred is his benchmark. In fact he believes that if the Cubs ever do win the World Series most of their fans will disappear. This unimportant losing in terms of real life provides an outlet for millions of people who follow the team. They are able to experience pain and loss without any serious consequences. This possibly helps them deal with life's more painful calamities. At least that is the party line Dirt's sticking with this fall. Next year he'll come up with another reason why none of this horrendous activity at Wrigley Field and other National League environs matters to him. I know better. He plans to watch the last seven games on TV at the bar. A less-than-restrained vigil in the offing. Visions of drink orders unfilled, wild gesticulations and foul oaths loomed on the horizon. We're an easily amused bunch in Beiderbeck.

Liz told me that she needed a few days to take care of some personal business such as visiting Sam and speaking with Moryn about what steps to take concerning her husband. Where should he be moved once the legal proceedings ran their course? His attorney told her that it appeared that Sam would never stand trial and probably that there is a strong chance that the court will order him confined to a mental institution for years if not the rest of his life, most likely at Turbid Springs. Her lawyer said that he's friends with the judge in this case and he that he will try to convince her that Sam will be better off in a private facility. He mentioned a place outside of Gillette, Wyoming. Their insurance will cover the expenses. If this happens, the state of Montana will have one less disturbed person on its hands. She also needs time to go through the house collecting Sam's things, guns, fly rods, photos, clothes and the like. She's committed to moving on and is planning to store his possessions at a place in town. She keeps saying that she will always love him. Often she spays these words through her tears, but what can she do? I doubt that he's ever going to get any better. More than likely Sam will never be turned free. He scarcely recognizes her anymore. Perhaps people will call her "a cold, calculating bitch," but she is determined to do what she believes is best for everyone including herself. She wants to spend the rest of her life doing productive, creative things, hopefully with someone she loves and I'd like to think that this individual could be me. At least that's what she tells me, and I'm inclined to believe her, perhaps because of the old 'love is blind' cliché. Whatever.

I don't care right now. She added that she's not going to waste the remaining years moping and wallowing in self pity. I admire her approach and her inner strength, even if this admiration is at least slightly fueled by my growing feelings for her.

I decide to use the time tying up loose ends with my business, paying some bills and finishing an article on carp fishing in the West for Fly Rod & Reel's. The magazine pays next to nothing like most of the other fly fishing books, but I can always use a few hundred extra dollars. Getting paid, even paid pocket change, for fishing and then writing about my often chaotic experiences, isn't all bad. Writing keeps me busy during a few of my slow hours and, in turn, out of trouble. If FR&R rejects the piece, I'll spin it off to a hook-and-bullet publication for big bucks, say two or three-hundred. At least the money will keep me in gas and coffee for a few weeks.

I was halfway through the story, describing in tediously exacting detail, as is expected in this type of work, a fly pattern I've invented that resembles a dough ball, the classic carp bait of all time. The thing works, taking a number of the fat cyprinids in the Little Missouri over by Alzada. I call the pattern Ed's Whiskey River. Maybe I'll get a patent on it so no one else could steal my design and make millions of dollars. While banging away at the laptop the Count bursts through the door still wearing his Octoberfest attire, though with a different pair of suspenders. This time the pattern is a series of Koala bears perched in Eucalyptus trees. His face is flushed and he's more animated than usual, which means borderline incoherent.

"Damn you, Bouchee. You've got to listen to me on this one. You absolutely must." He zeroes in on the refrigerator, tears the door open and grabs an Old Milwaukee, thankfully the last can. He pops the lid, drains the thing in one take and reaches for another, this time a bottle of Special Export. Normally the refrigerator contains at least two dozen different brands of beer and related beverages that have accrued over time and the course of numerous fishing and bird hunting outings. If variety is the spice of life, the fridge is that cliché's Mecca.

"I just got off the phone with my Siksika friend. He told me that the tribe is conducting an investigation into their buffalo herd. Actually it's ..." and he puts a hand up to quiet me before I even got started. "Merely testing you old boy to see if you are listening. I know all about Sam Jones and his favorite phrase. Liz told me ages ago. Old news dies hard with you, my laconic friend."

I sink back in my chair, move the cursor on the laptop to save, push the button and turn the machine off.

"While you're up Count, grab me a beer, will you?" He does, handing me a frosty and hefty can of Foster's Ale. "So what's up with the Siksikas?"

"Well some of them, my friend included, went out to check on the herd and see for themselves how it was fairing last week. They were shocked to discover that there were only fifty or sixty buffalo. And they were unable to find any small bands holding down out of the wind in the creek bottoms. They are going to get to the bottom of all this. Right now my friend said that his people are focusing their attention on the herd manager, someone named Grover Loudermilk. Hell of a name if you ask me. And that they are asking certain members of the tribal council some blunt questions. My friend is outraged. I've never heard him sound so exercised. Heads will roll on this one...or scalps will fly Take my word for it."

My stomach tightens at this. I've about finished with looking into Grace's murder. In fact, I figured that I was done with the matter. I'm not going to bill Liz for my time and expenses. The folder on the case is in order and lying on top of the file cabinet waiting to be put away. Now the Count's news.

"That's not the pithy portion of all of this, my friend." The Count kills his beer and tossed the can into a wastebasket by my desk. "My friend, who asks to remain nameless, at least at this juncture, said that he found part of a buffalo tail, one that had been severed near the tip with a knife from the looks of it, lying on the ground near an old fence post. From his description it sounds quite similar to the one you have there on your desk. What do you think of that?"

My stomach really became tight and my mind is starting to race at an uncommon velocity. Damn! I don't want to go back into this mess again, especially now that things are going so well between Liz and I. I don't want to upset her while she's putting her life in order. But the Count's news gets me going again, and I am someone who has a very hard time leaving anything unfinished.

"Here, let me dial my tribal friend. He won't give you his name, but ask him about the tail." He speaks briefly with someone on the phone, then hands it to me.

"This is Bouchee. I'm the one that's been looking into the Mark Grace killing down here for Sam Jones' wife," and we go back-and-forth filling each other in on minor points. The Count's friend knows all about the case, but then who doesn't. The story has dominated all the state media for weeks and flashed across the national airwaves Briefly when the news broke. In closing, I describe the tail I have to this man. He goes silent at this, then slowly says.

"I have no way of making you believe me, but that part of a tail sitting on the corner of your desk is from a slaughtered member of our herd. You will have to take my word on this. Some things are just known and cannot be explained. What I see is real. I know. And one more thing. Be careful if you go on with this. Death is all around you. That death can take many shapes. Many unusual shapes." The line goes dead. Only a dial tone.

I look up at the Count. He nods.

"Now do you see. Will you finally listen and take me seriously, and maybe actually follow up on this?" I say yes I will, but tell him I need some time alone to think about all of this before deciding what to do. The Count indicates that he understands perfectly, before standing up and bowing slightly before walking out the door. And he's gone just like he's never been here standing in front of me in the first place. This type of vanishing act is happening all too often these days to make me comfortable. I let The Dog out so that he can trot across the street and hang out at Ron Santo's barbershop, a daily ritual for both of them. I open another Foster's and take a drink. Truly a fine example of the brewer's art. A nice blend of hops, yeast and various grains with a nice carbonation. Ale doesn't get any better, and I realizing that I'm avoiding the issue here. Leaning back in my chair I smoke some cigarettes and sip my beer.

All through this thing, ever since the tail turned up, my instincts have been telling me that there is something strange to the case, awful even beyond the gruesome murder. The tail truly is the key, but where do I start. While going over my conversation with the member of the Siksikas I stare at the mangy piece of buffalo tail sitting on the corner my desk.

"On the corner of your desk," that's what the Count's tribal friend had said. Not that the buffalo tail is in my possession or the tail I have in my possession, but "On the corner of your desk." How does he know this? And I replay what else he said. "Some things are just known and cannot be explained," and last of all, "Death is all around you and it can take many shapes. Many unusual shapes."

~ ~ ~

Later that day I stop in at the Mint Bar in Davisville for a burger and a beer before I head up the Indian Creek road. The bar is a bit on the seedy side of things and caters to hard-core slammers. The ones that stagger in at eight in the morning with the shakes and stink of stale sweat and booze. The ones who need two hands or a straw to suck down the first couple of drinks of the day. A tough way to be. A hard way to live. I don't wish this on anyone. All in all a joyful joint.. The bartender is a stubby, bearded guy with a florid complexion known as Gabby. You know that he's a professional boozer, a pro's pro, by looking at his nose, bulbous, far out of proportion with the rest of his features and the burst veins on the thing looked like a confused road map coming and going from oblivion. Sometimes the place reeks of disinfectant and stale beer, but that is usually in the morning before business picks up.

Right now, by late afternoon, the aroma is a mixture of smoke, the grill and bar whiskey. Much better. Putting aside all of this, the Mint serves one of the best burgers in the country, a half-pound of ground, select sirloin topped with grilled home grown onions, tomato, lettuce, New York state sharp white cheddar and homemade garlic mayonnaise. The Kaiser roll is also homemade. So for four bucks, the price includes a mug of Ranier, a person can have himself a dandy lunch. I've been known to have two burgers after a long day chasing brown trout in the area. Once I ate three but all of the blood drained out of my head and down to my stomach where help was desperately needed. I had to lurch over to a booth and collect myself before driving back to town. The record is six, but that guy, Kerry Wood, died of a heart attack a year ago while putting up his second cut of hay in the August heat. So, two's my limit.

While waiting on my meal I eavesdrop on the conversation going on between a few of the boys seated next to me. They are talking loudly and laughing madly about someone they know who never has to worry about having any more children. From what I can gather the poor fellow was using a winch mounted on the front of his truck to pull a boulder out of the road leading to his home. Apparently the cable snapped and eliminated the part of his anatomy required for procreation. In a way I can see the undeniable mirth in this curious incident, but I would hate to experience a similar fate. I guess the individual is fortunate that he's alive and not whip sawed into two pieces. Bar humor. At its best it's pathetic, at its worst it's grim.

My burger arrives. I heft the huge sandwich in both hands. Mayonnaise and tomato slide down my chin and drip on the bar with the first bite. Delicious but the meat needs more salt. I undress the burger and start to sprinkle the salt. The shaker's lid falls off and an ounce of the white crystals pour out. The boys at the bar find this hilarious giving me the benefit of their scintillating wit. Comments run along the lines of "Salty enough for ya?" and "Have a little beef with your salt." These guys are quick. I dust off the burger and carry on.

As I'm finishing up my meal, a tall, lean figure walks in. Several inches taller than I was, the man had long, dark hair and a full beard. He blocks out most of the light coming in from the doorway. He asks for a couple of packs of Luckies.

"Coming right up, Mr. Miskis," says Gabby as he hustles to the cigarette shelf on the wall behind him. He pulls out to packs and hands them to this Miskis guy, who takes them. They disappear into a long, large, sun-browned hand and then into his red-and-black plaid wool coat.

He reaches into his jeans pocket and pulls out a thick roll of bills. As he does so a cylindrical, dark object drops to the floor, landing unnoticed by him in the bar detritus of peanut shells, road grit and cigarette butts. Before I can say anything, he's out the door, back in his truck and heading down the highway. I bend over to pick up whatever he's dropped. I stop halfway there like I've run into a brick wall.

Lying amid the junk and sawdust is the tip of a buffalo tail. Another one making an appearance in my life. I almost fall on the floor. One more damn buffalo tail.

~ ~ ~

I turn on to the Indian Creek Road now in search of someone called Miskis. No first name. No last. The buffalo tail is far too much of a sign to be written off as mere coincidence. The guy in The Mint looks tough and plenty capably of taking care of himself. After I found the tail on the bar floor, I finished my beer and ordered another. Instead of rushing out the door and following the guy, I wanted to collect myself, to calm down and try and think things through. If the man is who I think he is, he's a killer and a calculatingly, ruthless one at that. I casually ask the bartender who the guy is who just bought the Luckies. He leans over close to me, placing his hands on the low bar.

"Name's Miskis. Just the one name. No first or maybe it's no last name. And I don't know much about him." I'm treated to Gabby's breath smelling of whiskey, beer, onions and cigars. "Lives way up Injun Crick, off a ways on that dirt road, if you could call the piece of rutted shit a road. You know, the one that cuts left just beyond the old barn 'bout fifteen miles, give or take, from the highway?"

I say that I do know. He moves off to visit with the crew down the bar. What should I do? Logic and common sense mixed in with a faint sense of self preservation clearly says that it's something that I know I'll never do - head back to Biederbeck and tell Qualls what I've discovered. The smart play, one I unfortunately rarely make, is to let him and his officers take care of things. But that's not who I am. Taking on bad, twisted cases, falling in love with a very troubled woman who's still married and riding every edge I can find, that's who I am all too often.

There's a reason why I'm nearly always broke, divorced and will probably never write a great novel. Taking risks seems the only way to live for me. Started one August when I was five and found out my parents were separating, so I decided, the hell with them and left home to go live down along the river beneath some willow trees. Lasted for the better part of the day before I came straggling back. I'd given it my best shot and gotten my first taste, in a small way, of acting on impulse. Lot of painful mistakes from there to here. So what? In the process I've experienced some wild times and done a few things most people would never think of, let alone consider if they did. So I decide to seek out Miskis and perhaps ask him a few questions.

Gabby's right, the road to Miskis's place isn't much, a piece of rutted shit like the bartender said it was, but it was easy to find, too, running off to the left across the stream and up over some low hills. I bounce along slowly wondering what I'm doing and what Miskis will say or, of greater concern, do. Coming to the top of a rise I can just make out his cabin in the gathering darkness. The truck's headlights flash across a dilapidated barn and an old shed. I can see Miskis's truck inside, at least the bed with a gray tarp covering whatever is stored beneath. I ease into the yard and turn off the engine. No time like the present I think lamely, so I get out and start to approach the place. Miskis comes through the door looking huge, menacing, like the grim reaper Montana style. He's not smiling. He stops abruptly. So do I. We stare at each other for what seems like a long time, but is most likely only a couple of seconds. I feel weak, drained of all energy and will. I can't speak. The feel of danger, violence and my fear are thick right now at this place. A slight shift and glow in his eyes tells me that Miskis senses this, too.

Then from somewhere far away, Wyoming?, I hear my voice say, "I'm Ed Bouchee, a private detective looking into the murder of Mark Grace for someone. Maybe you've heard of her. She lives down in Coltrane. Liz Jones." I don't have a clue about what's going to happen next. "I saw you today at The Mint. The bartender told me you lived up here and how to find your place. I thought you might have seen or heard something that might help me. That might help Ms. Jones."

Miskis reaches for something in his coat pocket. I think about running, but instead of a pistol, he pulls out a new pack of Luckies, opens it and lights up.

"Don't know the name," he says. "Come in anyway. Long way up here. Shot of whiskey will help your drive back," and he heads back inside. I notice that his right hand is fumbling around in the pocket. Probably trying to find the tail. I'm scared senseless, like when I've been caught on a narrow, cliff-face trail hanging a thousand feet above a creek that looks like a silver string from my vertiginous location. I'm barely able to make my feet work. When I walk into the kitchen he's already sitting down. Two glasses of whiskey are waiting, the amber liquid shining darkly. A kerosene lantern gives the room its only light. I sit down, reach for my glass and manage to keep my hand from shaking. His hands, dark and weathered, are resting on the table. On the right one is a large gold ring with a large sapphire. Familiar, then I remember Grace always flashing a ring like that around town. Not like that. Miskis is wearing Grace's ring. I'm sitting across the table from his killer. I figure I'm dead now, too.

"That murder was an ugly deal," says Miskis as he eyes me over the top of his glass. "But I don't know a thing about it. Keep to myself up here. Works out better. Can't help you out. Drink your drink and be on your way."

I see a shotgun and a rifle standing in a corner behind a wooden stove that is cranking out the heat. I do as I'm told and drink my drink. The stuff burns all the way down to my stomach, which feels very good right now. Miskis watches me the whole time. Then it hits me in long-distance, time-delayed recall. He's the man I spotted standing in the middle of Indian Creek that time The Dog and I drove up to examine the murder site. I'm certain that he's going to kill me at any second. I decide to try and make a calm exit. There aren't any other options. I stand up, which is a noble effort on my part considering the fact that my knees are like worn our rubber bands at the moment. I can't feel my legs and I'm not all that sure that they're still connected to the rest of me. I am terrified. That's all I can feel. Absolute fear firing through my nerves and racing around in my head. No thought. Nothing else. Only terror. The place and this man radiate hate and malevolence, and there is something else in the air. A soft, musky scent I've smelled before. Then what is really going on explodes in my brain. What I smell is First, the perfume Liz wears. Damn. Miskis. Another part of a buffalo tail. Grace's ring. Now Liz's perfume.

I try to hold things together saying "Thanks for the drink." I turn my back on Miskis and hear him rise, both the wooden chair and floor boards creaking with the movement, a lethal sound to me right now. I'm going to be murdered. I can feel it, like a high from losing control of my truck on a patch of black ice with a semi bearing down on me in the opposite lane. I keep walking, out the door and over the long yards to my truck. This takes forever, the longest experience in my life. I'm sure that a bullet is going to blast into the back of my skull any second now. Then I'm in my truck. I hear the engine turn over and catch, sounding better than any music I've ever listened to. I shift into first, swing around and start back down to the Indian Creek Road. I never look back at Miskis. In the side mirror I see him standing back there by the door. As soon as I'm out of sight of his place, I drive as hard and fast as I can. I stop back at the Mint.

"A double Beam, Gabby and a glass of beer."

He brings them, looks at me, decides he doesn't like what he sees, says "On the house, Bouchee," and goes back to playing cribbage with his friends at the other end of the bar. I finish the drinks and head for the Biederbeck police station and Jim Qualls.

~ ~ ~

Liz passes Bouchee on the highway as he hurries back to town. She recognizes his truck by the fact that the left-side headlight is out and by the three small orange and two red lights that are visible on the roof just above the windshield. No one else she knows has anything like that on their truck, especially with the headlight gone. She can't see inside the cab because of the lack of light, but she's certain that it's Bouchee. He probably didn't notice her driving the other way in the darkness. Even if it was broad daylight, how could he at the speed he's going? Seeing him roar past at what seems close to ninety, she knows intuitively that he's figured things out. That realization comes through clearly.

"Damnit all to hell," she says to herself.

She hurries on to the cabin. When she walks in the front door Miskis is sitting there in the kitchen smoking, a glass of whiskey in front of him. He's been waiting for her. Nothing ever really changes with him. Probably never will.

This time he speaks first, an unusual occurrence.

"Bouchee was here. He knows."

That's all.

He pours her a drink and slides the pack of smokes across the table. The whiskey calms her as does the cigarette, the smoke filling her lungs and giving her a nicotine rush. The two of them look at each. They both know what must be done. They are so close now, so much a part of each other. Spoken words are unnecessary. Still, Liz feels the need to talk. The sound of her voice reinforces the unspoken words that pass between them and help her visualize what is going on.

"I made a mistake hiring him in the first place. I really thought having him check into things would make things look good. Divert attention. I never thought he'd put all this together. But then I never figured that Sam would put all of this together and confront us here with Mark. And I never thought that Mark would go completely crazy and threaten to turn all of us, even himself, into the police. If he could have held things together for awhile longer I know I could have handled Sam until it was right for us to run up north for good, but then things never seem to go smoothly or the way they should in my life. We had to kill Mark and drive Sam way into one of his dark places, but I wish that we hadn't."

"They go the way they go for each of us," says Miskis. He sips his drink. "We're all dead from the moment we're born, some of us just happen to find out this fact sooner than others."

"Yes. I guess so. You're right as always," Liz says. "But once you realized that Bouchee had figured things out, why didn't you kill him and get rid of the truck. I can't believe I'm saying this. Killing people like having a drink. I like all three of them, love them each in their own ways, but I'm you now and your thoughts and actions are mine, too. Totally insane but completely sensible."

Miskis works on his drink, says nothing.

The line of reasoning is clearly pointless, even to Liz. Killing Bouchee, stashing his body and losing the truck somewhere would be no big thing in this vast, empty country. A dozen places come to mind. Up in the canyon along Sixteen Mile or far in The Breaks down some unnamed coulee or over in the badlands east of Glendive. The police would never find a trace of him, at least not for a long time, but she knows, as Miskis does, that this is only delaying the inevitable. They have to move on, out of the area, far away from Biederbeck. To be together all of the time physically, they must flee to someplace where no one knows either one of them.

Once Grace discovered the two of them in bed that night in June when he pulled up unexpectedly to talk with Miskis about maybe easing off on shooting the tribe's bison, everything was set in motion. Miskis made no attempt to buy Mark's silence. He'd been considering killing both he and Sam for months, figuring that Mark would eventually tell Sam what they were up to with the wild game, that is if he didn't figure things out on his own, which he did. He thought that some night when they were all drinking heavily around a campfire at the logging site. He'd backed away from killing people for some time. Not because he thought that murder was a matter of right or wrong. A serious need hadn't arisen, that's all. Not in terms of dealing with the day-to-day. Not yet. Instead, Miskis had tried to scare the two away from the Indian Creek drainage by making them think a large grizzly was in the area. He clawed their skidcat along with trees around camp with a mummified paw cut off a bear he'd killed in the Mission Mountains over to the West when he poached big game in that country. He killed that bear years ago for a rich stockbroker from back East, one who fancied himself a big-game hunter but didn't have the skill, stamina and, most importantly, the guts to shoot a grizzly up close himself. Miskis made ten thousand on that one. He used the paw to make tracks around camp, skillfully and randomly. He trashed the camp a few times when the two weren't around. What he hadn't figured into the equation was that Sam was so close to the edge to begin with and that he'd put all of it together. He was unable to drive the two away, but at this point any slight weirdness, anything anomalous in Sam's distraught life carried far more weight than it would have with someone else. Someone a bit more stable. By the time Grace caught Liz and Miskis, her husband was driven by extreme anxiety and confusion. All the years of drinking and spending time with the dark side of life had worn him down. Plus he knew that Liz was seeing someone else, that she no longer loved him as her husband. He began to wonder if she ever had.

So when Grace walked in that night, Miskis took a big risk. He poured Grace a drink and when he wasn't looking he knocked Grace out by slamming the butt of the shotgun into the back of his head. Then he and Liz tied up the body, loaded it in the back of her Landcruiser and drove up to the logging site. Without discussing their plans, the two knew what they were going to do. When they pulled up they saw Sam sitting on a stump clutching a whiskey bottle. His head was bent down to his chest. The two of them walked up to Sam. He slowly looked up at them, finally recognizing first Liz then Miskis. He tried to say something, but no words came out of his mouth. Then they undressed and made love in front of Sam. Liz was now so completely one with Miskis, that everything they did or thought together seemed right. He watched and listened to his wife moan with pleasure. He heard Miskis's rough, animal grunts, but he never left his stump. Then Miskis and Liz went back to the Landcruiser, still naked and covered with sweat, dirt and pine needles. They picked up Grace, who was coming around by this time, and dragged him to the fire ring. What happened next really did push Sam over the edge. What was done would have driven most people mad. He went over to Sam's truck and returned wearing a pair of work gloves and carrying Sam's Stihl chainsaw. He pulled the cord and revved the machine into a deafening roar. But before Miskis could use the machine Liz stepped forward from the shadows, grabbed the saw and cut Grace in half herself. Miskis completed the ghastly work by cutting Mark's head off and quartering the body. There was no thought in her actions just like Miskis. She'd turned a dark corner and walked into a country where right and wrong no longer existed, only the entity that Miskis and Liz had become. Feelings from her past, feelings for those she knew, disappeared. She was now an outlaw in the purest and highest sense. Society, morals, rules, none of this existed in her world anymore. Hacking up Grace was something that needed doing in as harsh and brutal way as possible if the two of them were to insure that that insanity spike was truly driven home in Sam's head. Miskis's eyes grew darker still, illuminated with a blackness that came from unconsciously feeding on another ravaged souls. Naturally giving in to the evil that resided within them, within all of us, had set them free forever. They would always be together no matter what happened. Their love was an elevated form of insanity, perhaps a super sanity beyond the ability of normal men to comprehend.

Sam, now also dripping with his friend's blood, relinquished what little grip he had on linear motion and conventional reality, not like Miskis and his wife, but in an uncontrollable, horrifying way where time had no meaning, and peace and serenity were non-existent. He was in an abject horror show with no concept of redemption. Sam was now a permanent resident of an insane landscape peopled with his own relentless demons. Screaming, moaning, sobbing and finally going silent. Sam watched as the two dug a grave nearby and dropped his friend's remains in the hole. But before this was done, Miskis pulled the sapphire ring from the dead hand, gave it Liz and said "Place this on my finger." She did as Miskis forced her to maintain eye contact. After they filled in the grave, they went to the creek and washed off the dirt and gore. Next they smoothed over all of their tracks with pine boughs. They turned to Sam. He remained quiet and motionless staring at Mark's grave, but seeing nothing. He was gone. Killing him would not serve their needs. Another murder was not needed. He was the perfect foil to take the heat for their killing. They left the chainsaw between the grave and the fire, then got dressed and drove back to the cabin confident that whatever Sam told the police when the murder was eventually discovered, wouldn't be believed. They were sure that the cops would charge Sam with Grace's murder and that he would eventually be convicted and confined either in prison or a mental institution for life.

But Miskis made one mistake. One he was unaware of. He dropped one of the buffalo tails that he always carried with him. The stub fell into some brush that grew thickly around the campsite. It had dropped from his coat pocket when he'd flung off his clothes. The tails prove to be the keys to the murder, the one left at the murder scene, the one on the Siksika Reservation and the one at The Mint Bar in Davisville. His obsession with those tails is an error, the kind he's never made before. For a man who never makes mistakes, to do so three times in basically the same fashion is an indication of the awesome justness and power of fate. Life can be that way at times. Fix on something and it becomes commonplace and finally turns invisible, unnoticed by that person, but still there none the less, all of the while delicately influencing life's seemingly haphazard chain of events. Fate is as permanent and inevitable as gravity or friction. Immutable forces that direct all life on the planet.

Miskis and Liz would have been home free, except for those buffalo tails. One found by itself would have meant nothing, maybe even two, but all three revealed far too much in many subtle and not so subtle forms. They turned everything the wrong way. Now the two of them had to run. The stocks that she and Sam held together would have to wait, maybe forever. She had planned to sell them off after Sam was legally declared incompetent to handle his own affairs, a time when she would gain the power of attorney for her husband, but for now that money was out of reach. Still, between them they had well over a quarter-million in cash stored in the cabin. Money from the wild game he'd sold and from cash she'd accumulated by slowly selling off some stocks and bonds she'd inherited from her father year's ago. With that kind of money, she thought, we can run into Canada, maybe way up north in the Peel River Country near the Arctic Circle in the Yukon. She'd been up that way a couple of times in her teens with her father as he walked the forests and mountains for days hunting Dall rams in the unexplored mountains that rolled off in all directions range upon range. No one would find them up that way. Because Miskis had been there a few years back, saying that it was still wild and an easy place to disappear into, they both immediately agreed on the location. They could drop from sight up there.

"That will work," said Miskis. "That will work fine."

So Liz explained her plan to Miskis. He already knew what they were going to do, but he understood her need to tell him about how she was going drive back to Coltrane and grab what she needed, mostly clothes and then meet him back here in a couple of hours, shortly before dawn. They'd leave the Landcruiser at the murder site, causing some confusion when the cops arrived, probably not long after they discovered this cabin abandoned. That would buy them time. They'd take his truck along back roads and cross into Canada at the out-of-the-way Port of Whitlash on the northern side of The Sweet Grass Hills. No one lived up there. That crossing was a cinch. They would be over the border before word went out. From there they'd take it easy, moving cautiously along less-traveled roads as they worked their way north up through Rocky Mountain House and Grande Cache in Alberta, then through Dawson Creek and Fort Liard in British Columbia and finally up through Watson Lake, Teslin and Whitehorse in the Yukon. They could do it if they kept low, well below the notice of the authorities radar, radar that was light the farther north one traveled. It could work. They both knew there was a strong chance of them gaining their anonymity and attendant freedom in the Canadian Northwest.

She gets up and looks at Miskis. He returns her internal fire that radiates from his eyes. This time they really are one being. Where she stops and he starts - that distinction is obliterated. She goes outside and drives back to her house. Miskis gets up with the intention of going to the creek and pulling out the net. Why? He doesn't know. It's something he needs to do. That's all. Everything they need up north is already either in the cab of the truck or stowed away under a tarp in the bed. He grabs his 30.30 and starts to walk out, but stops. He stands in place for a long time, then turns around. He sits down at the table, laying the rifle across it. And he waits. For what, he has no idea nor does he care. Why he's waiting is unimportant. He just is. That's all, again.

~ ~ ~

I pull up to the police station, stop abruptly, push through the doors and go looking for Qualls. I'm sure I appear three-quarters nuts – wild-eyed, hair going in every direction like Einstein's.

"Where is he?" I ask the ever-present Ginny who's now reading *Eastertown* by Max Crawford. Gutsy lady.

She looks up.

"Oh my God."

She leads me by the arm to a chair. I sit down, collapsing like a cheap lawn chair that can't handle the weight anymore.

"Where is he?" I ask again.

She steams over to the large metal coffee pot and quickly returns with a cup of her infamous brew. Salvation is at hand. I take a drink. At this point, even with whipping cream and sugar, the salty liquid tastes damn good.

"Where is he?" I almost yell. "I've got to talk with Qualls right now."

"Hold on," she says. "He went over to Ray's to have a drink with Dirt." She calls over there, speaks briefly, then clicks off. "He and Dirt will be right here. Jim said for you to wait in his office and to stay put."

I do as I'm told. Where does he think I'm going anyway? I'm exhausted, still half terrified to death and a man with important information concerning a murder. In two minutes Qualls comes through the door with Dirt huffing and puffing behind him.

"Bouchee. What in the hell happened? What's going on? You wreck your truck again?"

The two of them stand there looking at me like I'm the lone survivor of some hideous Mexican bus crash down the side of a mountain in the Sierra Madre Oriental. I take another blast of coffee and hold out my mug for more. Dirt takes it from my hands and heads for the sacred urn. Qualls walks over and sits down behind his desk. Dirt returns with mugs for each of us and sits down beside me.

"Now tell me what's going on. You look like you've been through all kinds of bullshit," says Qualls with a quick nod to Dirt, who's looking at me with concern.

I try to gather myself by taking a couple of deep breaths. I'd read somewhere that this is supposed to calm the nerves. No dice. I begin anyway, starting from the day when Liz first walked into my office. I tell them everything in detail, relying on my crack memory. Everything except some of the intimate details of my supposed love affair with Liz. I now believe that I've been taken for a serious ride on this one. Nothing gets by me. I now know better than to think love really exists in the new millennium. I remember that Joe Jackson wrote a little number about fools in love. I should have played the CD months ago. This one will hurt like hell for weeks with a gnawing, persistent ache in the pit of my stomach complete with self-recrimination for being a fool, total lassitude and, quite possibly, a bit too much whiskey for awhile. That fun will all come down on me later, when this was over. I started telling them what I know shortly before two a.m. and finish up about 3:45. The clincher is when I tell them that Miskis is wearing Grace's sapphire ring. That's when

Qualls asks me if I think Miskis is still at the cabin.

"Beats the hell out of me, Jim," I say. "No way can I figure that guy or what he might do. He's dangerous, unpredictable and obviously ruthless."

He calls the county judge at home, apologizes for waking him, explains the situation and says that he needs a warrant for Miskis's arrest right now and another one for Liz Jones. Qualls and the judge are old friends, so the half-awake man says he'll have both documents ready for him in 45 minutes. Next he calls a bunch of people including the Fish and Wildlife Service, the Forest Service, state and county authorities, and Biederbeck senior officer George Mitterwald. He accurately and succinctly fills each of them in on what I've just recounted. Then there is a bunch of calls coming in, and several going out that are made by Qualls. I'm coming down from my encounter with Miskis and things around me aren't registering with a great deal of clarity. I gather that the various agencies are coordinating their forces for a pre-dawn raid at Miskis's cabin. By a little after five everything was in place. that everyone is going to rendezvous at the turnoff to Indian Creek. There's about an hour-and-a-half until daybreak. If all of the people involved drive like maniacs from their various locations scattered around the county, they just make all get there by sunrise. No one is really in charge, maybe Qualls, that sort of procedural thing never counted for much in this part of the country. Taking care of business, what needs to be done, is what matters with people around here. Unless some FBI big shots wander over from Billings to stick their noses in Biederbeck business either out of boredom or perhaps morbid curiosity, all of the local and state agencies get along together fine. The shelter of dark would have been better, but the half light of dawn will have to do. Miskis can head out for points unknown at any time. He may have already done so. Qualls mentions that he's learned from Fish, Wildlife and Park license records that Miskis's first name is Ed. Just like me. How nice all of this is.

"Dirt, keep an eye on him until we get back," says Qualls as he points to me.

"Bullshit, too. I'm going up there one way or the other. Don't try and stop me. Not on this one. No damn way."

I mean it.

Qualls looks at me, shakes his head and turns back to Dirt.

"You drive and stay well behind me, and keep him under control. Damn, when he gets this worked up there's no telling what he'll do. The last time he was even close to being this crazy, he drove his truck through the front door of the Mini Mart. And just what in the hell was that all about anyway? Never mind. I don't want to know."

"I remember that one, and trust me, you don't want to know," says Dirt. "I'll do my best." He grabs my arm firmly and adds "Keep a lid on things, Eddie boy. Promise me."

I do. I hope I can.

The three of us head off in search of Miskis.

~ ~ ~

We're gathered in the early-morning dark at the turnoff near Davisville. There are trucks, squad cars and Dirt's Oldsmobile. Men dressed in various agency uniforms mill about drinking coffee and smoking cigarettes, or stand silently by themselves scuffing the dirt.

Everyone is aware that something serious is about to take place, that some of them might be shot or killed. The mood is nervous, excited and cautious. Qualls calls everyone together and outlines the plan of attack. Not much of a plan, but what can he do? Essentially we all drive up to Miskis's cabin, surround the place and then order him to surrender, which none of us thinks for a moment he'll do. Anyone who kills a man and cuts him into pieces probably doesn't think too highly of the law or human life, including his own. And there's the possibility that Liz is there with him. There are a few questions like should they shoot to kill, and if so, on whose command. Qualls, thinks for a moment, then says "Yes" to the first question and also says that he'll be the one to give the order. Then we all get back in our vehicles and head up the road to Lord only knows what.

~ ~ ~

All of us are in place now. Over twenty armed men surround the cabin, concealing themselves behind rocks, deadfalls and large Ponderosa pines. Dirt and I are farther back, out of the line of fire about a half-mile from where we all parked, holding where Qualls told us to. We're still close enough to see the cabin and the faint glow of light coming from the windows of the place. Qualls gives everybody time to settle in, then stands up and raises a bullhorn to his mouth.

"Ed Miskis, this is Jim Qualls of the Biederbeck police department. I have a warrant for your arrest charging you with the murder of Mark Grace. Come out and surrender. You are surrounded by armed members of the law." He waits, turns to Mitterwald and says in a low voice, "I've never done this before. Sounded as half-ass as that junk on TV." He smiles and shrugs his shoulders.

Mitterwald returns the smile, raises his hands palms up and says "What else was there to say?"

Qualls turns back to the cabin.

No sign of Miskis. Or Liz. No sign of life period. Qualls repeats his statement and waits again. Still nothing. He tries one more time and when still more nothing happens, he speaks into his hand-held radio and orders the men to move in, slowly. All of them begin to creep towards the cabin, crouching low and using even the smallest bush or rock for cover in the growing light. The sky over the mountains is becoming brighter with the approaching sunrise, but clouds are also moving in. Heavy, dark ones that mean rain. Qualls then orders one of his men to lob canisters of tear gas into the cabin. The first two miss, landing on the roof above the kitchen window then falling to the ground. They begin smoking with a hissing sound of escaping gas. The third one crashes through the glass. Still there's no movement inside. Qualls then orders the men to move closer. When they are within twenty yards the light goes out in the cabin and a tall, dark figure runs out the door. Qualls yells for Miskis to stop, but instead he turns in the direction of the voice and levers off several rounds, one tearing into Mitterwald's arm. No order to fire is needed. Everyone shoots at what they think is Miskis, who continues running for the trees that were off in the direction of The Nortons, and fairly close to the cabin. At first he moves swiftly with a fluidity of a trained athlete, surprisingly agile for such a big man. He stumbles once, possibly from being hit, fires several more times at two men in his way, dropping both of them and disappears into the forest. Qualls yells through the bullhorn for everyone to stop shooting. He has to do this several times before the firing ceases. The air is thick with smoke from all the gunfire. The silence is loud without the shooting.

A flickering orange glow comes from inside the cabin. A fire is spreading, probably started by the heat of the tear gas canister. Qualls tells one of the men to call in the firefighting aircraft that is on call and loaded with fire retardant to put the thing out before the blaze spreads to the dry forest. It starts to rain, but he's taking no chances. The last thing he needs here is a forest fire that after the hot, dry summer will explode like a bomb and tear through thousands of acres of timber. Besides Mitterwald, four other men are wounded, the two that blocked Miskis's path seem to be in bad shape. Two others over by the shed both have leg wounds. While they're attended to by paramedics that have been standing by right next to Dirt and I, Qualls talks to a member of the Forest Service who knows the lay of the land here, asking him what their next move should be. The guy says that finding Miskis in this stuff with the lowering weather would be a "Bitch."

Dirt and I approached.

Qualls looks at me. He was not a happy man. Despite the best preparations possible under the time constraint, they've blown it. Men have been hurt, possibly mortally.

"I have no idea where the hell he went," he says to us. "We've lost him. No shit, Jimmy boy. We've damn well lost him. Great job." Qualls kicks at the ground and then looks off into the dense forest.

We stand there like dummies when out of the blue the

picture of Miskis standing in the stream near the murder scene flashes in front of me like a holographic projection from some Sci-Fi TV series. I tell Qualls about what I'd seen weeks ago, what I'm thinking and he remembers my telling him some of this a few hours earlier.

"Hunches are for losers, but what have we got to lose," he says. He rounds up a number of the men and we run back to the parking area, headed for the logging site. The sound of an airplane heading our way drones in the distance. Dirt and I jump in the GMC Jimmy with Qualls. He doesn't say anything, but, rather, drives like a madman determined to die a mangled death, covering the distance to where I remember seeing Miskis in an apoplectic heartbeat. It is now daylight.

"Slow down, I think it's right around this bend, just below that bunch of aspens."

We stop right there and get out, seeking cover anywhere it presents itself. We move slowly in the rain, and with extreme caution towards the place I have in mind. And there he was, standing once again in the middle of Indian Creek by what looks like a net. Even from a hundred yards away you can see the brown trout stuck in the mesh. Miskis is madly ripping the fish from the net and throwing them up on the far bank. Instead of running for freedom back in the mountains, he's down in the creek dealing with brown trout. I don't have a clue on this one. Miskis must be crazy. Completely nuts. Anyone else would be running for the high country and a place to hide until nightfall when he could make a break out of the region. Not this guy. He's down there ripping trout from a net like that's the only game in town.

It seemed that everyone begins firing at once, the bullets slamming Miskis into the net. He looks our way briefly as another volley of fire tears into him. Even at this distance I can feel the deadly heat of his gaze. The mangled body crumples, falling over the top of the net. The struggling of the trapped fish combines with the force of the stream's current to twist Miskis around and around. His lifeless body wraps tightly in his own net, surrounded by hundreds of thrashing, confused fish. I see blood draining out of Miskis and seeping into Indian Creek and drifting down stream in long strings that fade as they mix with the river's current.

We all look at each other, speechless.

What was there to say?

~ ~ ~

The corpse wriggles and flops in a grotesque parody of life. Hundreds of frantic fish thrash around in the partially submerged net. The small stream's current surges against the big trout as they pile up against the thick mesh. Sporadically the water, backed up by the body and the trapped fish, pulses over the top of the net carrying fat brown trout and some Yellowstone cutthroat trout with it in a wild rainbow rush of color downstream past moss-covered banks and beneath tall Ponderosa pines, small cedars growing in the shade of the old trees and thick clumps of tag alder and wild raspberries. Marauding dragonflies cruise the airwaves feeding on the slim dregs of this year's mosquito crop. The forest is muted in the dull light of the cold, drizzling day. Even the golds and yellows of the turning aspen leaves looked depressed, the trees gathered in small pockets of lifeless color growing along soft creases of the mountain's flank. Bull elk bugle back and forth in the open slopes of avalanche chutes far above the stream. The throaty, whistling sound of the animals rides eerily on the dank air.

Summer is dead.

So is Miskis.

Two Forest Service employees struggle with the water-logged body in the icy water. Hard work. Arms, legs and a torn ear are tangled in the nylon mesh. Hundreds of pounds of confused trout don't help either. The fish are trapped between this lower net, another one lashed to the trees on either side of the flow twenty yards above and the stumbling neoprene hip wader-covered legs of a bunch of law enforcement officials who scour the streambed and banks for shell casings and anything else related to the morning's violence. The brown trout only want to move far upstream to time-honored spawning gravels to pair up and breed. In human terms, it is last call at the local tavern and the prime choices are growing slimmer by the minute. Time to push on or face a lonely evening or in the case of the trout, a non-productive year. The cutthroat don't know what's going on, either. They spawn late in the spring, so the procreational urge isn't an issue with them. All their tiny brains can do is crazily flash signals of flee, run, hide to wildly twitching muscles. The whole scene is charged with an adrenaline rush of terrified confusion.

I try to remember all that I've been through in the last twenty-four hours, a period that feels like it started a thousand years ago. I try to remember and at the same time to forget all that has happened in the weeks leading up to this ugly morning.

Miskis's cabin is wrecked. The dousing with fire retardant dropped from the belly of the slurry bomber has crushed nearly flat what remains of the structure. The weight and force of the sticky stuff pounding down from several hundred feet has hammered the old building. The place was already badly wounded from the waves of gunfire that came from all directions. The job's been a thorough one in a misfiring, chaotic way. All of us have made sure that the fire and Miskis are dead out. I imagine what the cabin looks like right now. Shattered, charred siding, and splintered beams smoldering and steaming in a pile of twisted angles. The torched pickup with acrid fumes from the cooked tires will lend a nice touch. The stench of burned fish and wild game is mixing with the retardant and moist smoke, a scent that is unnatural, ugly, compared to the normally clear, pine-scented air in these mountains. I almost gag thinking about this.

Considering the mess I think 'Quite a damn spectacle for something as basic as murder, even the gruesome nature of this one. Of course there's still Miskis to factor in to the weird equation. He's been shot to pieces without any of us ever having the chance to ask him about all of this, any of this – the murder, he and Liz, his life. And several officers are wounded, though all are expected to survive. Sam Jones is under psychiatric care at Turbid Springs. There are also macabre aspects of all of this that I only dimly sense, let alone ever hope to understand.

"Man has Montana changed, " I mutter while firing up a Camel, the smoke from the cigarette mixing with the mayhem floating all around. "Damn do-gooders trying to finish off hunting and fishing, animal rights groups doing the same, and others want to eat real native Montana trout at their favorite restaurants. Won't touch beef. Wouldn't want to poison their systems with red meat. They even got that mall in Bozeman to remove the stuffed polar bear at the entrance. They said that it was a barbaric symbol that they couldn't tolerate, that the thing offended their delicate sensibilities. Too damn bad. They've trashed California and Colorado. Now they bring their selfish, destructive attitude up here. Bastards."

"What's that Eddie?" asks Dirt. "Everything comes back to your love for developers and the people they cater to these days, doesn't it? They're just a sign of the times. A passing phenomenon, like hippies and, praise the lord, disco music. Ease up and enjoy yourself more. Why fight what you can't change. Don't become one of those you detest. That would be the ultimate irony to some of us who know you."

"Maybe that guy on the stretcher there isn't as bad as some of the legal one's who are making a fortune at the last of the remaining good country's expense" I say and point the burning tip of my smoke at Miskis's mangled body as it passes by while being hauled to an ambulance. "All he did was clearly violate some fish and game Regs, kill Grace and perhaps a few others. Hell they do stuff a lot worse all the time in D.C. Too many of us around anyway. Damn dot-com millionaires and their invisible Internet fortunes ruin whatever they touch. Cigars. Fly fishing. Good country. It's discouraging."

The past weeks have worn me out. I'm beat. At this point I don't really care about anything except my need to be angry.

"Eddie, stay with the matter at hand. Leave the poor fools alone. They'll be gone soon enough or bunched up in Bozeman like sheep or in the nearby valleys and sterile developments. Winters up here will drive most of them off eventually. Snow, wind, cold. Not like the pictures the state puts out in its travel brochures. And we scare them, too. They never expected that kind of wild life. Bears and wolves, yes, but us? Good God. People that actually speak their minds. Biederbeck isn't Aspen. Except for eating at my place, they never come to town. Too rough. Too windy. Too strong a place. Relax. After we get a bunch of their money, we'll push them over to Idaho or Utah or maybe North Dakota. Those boys would find them most amusing. I know you're blown away by all of this today, but we better concentrate on things here and take a look at what's left of Miskis. I want to see if he's still wearing Grace's sapphire ring."

We walk over to the ambulance. I mumble a number of stupid things, but then I've been accused of being both a Neanderthal and a sleaze monger by critics of my writing so what the hell? The things I say are suggestions about what certain people can do with themselves, some quite creative and most likely illegal in many states. I'm just blowing off steam and don't even take myself seriously. Dirt, as good friends do, holds his tongue and only smiles a little bit at my last outburst. He's seen and heard all this once or twice before, even felt the same way, but is more restrained about such matters. He knows that venting off this anger keeps me from doing other more overt acts that would lead to trouble. That car-wrecked Mini Mart comes to mind.

Miskis is in bad shape. He is, after all, dead, but beyond that, the many rounds of rifle and handgun fire plus the deleterious effects of copper-plated buckshot have shredded his carcass.

But something catches all of our eyes. Something totally unexpected. An arrow is sticking into Miskis's chest, the other end protruding out his back and through his shirt. The arrowhead is hand-chipped obsidian and jet black. The three feathers near the notch look to be from an eagle. The shaft is hand worked and smoothed.

"Now where in God's name did this come from?" asks Qualls. "Don't touch that. Forensics needs to log all of this. Damn! Nothing happens as it should. A simple shootout and now we've got an Indian arrow to contend with."

Qualls looks at me, then walks up the bank to his rig.

Dirt bends down and looks at the man's right hand. Grace's ring is still on his middle finger. Three carats of Yogo sapphire found by Grace's grandfather one-hundred years ago at Kelly Coulee in central Montana's Little Belt Mountains. The gem has been cut and polished into blazing blue luminescence and then set in a ring made of gold dust panned in a Placer mine near Grasshopper Creek over by Bannack, One of a kind. Priceless in its own way. A piece of the state before the state was straightened, drawn-and-quartered and civilized by all of us. Dirt and I share a glance, a knowing look between old buddies that says more than words ever can. The damn ring symbolizes the madness of this deal as much as anything.

~ ~ ~

Liz reaches the turn-off just in time to see the long line of cars and trucks heading up the Indian Creek Road. She knows that their plans for escape to Canada are finished. She pulls over to the side of the road, turns off the engine and sits quietly with her eyes closed. Miskis's face appears, glowing silver against the blackness. She hears him say "It's over. I'll be dead soon. Then I'll be within you forever. Go back. Leave." His image fades in her mind. She looks up towards the east and sees peaks of The Nortons standing black against the star-filled sky. Clouds hung in a thick layer swirling around the middle of the mountains, but the tops poke through, the taller peaks rise for a thousand feet or more. A silver-blue aura shimmers along the ridgeline. The sun will be rising soon.

~ ~ ~

She knows now that he is dead. The moment the bullets ripped apart his heart a blinding white light blazed in front of her. Then she felt him inside of her. All of who he'd been or was still becoming is with her now. When the police show up she is waiting for them, sitting on the front porch smoking one of his cigarettes. They read her rights, place handcuffs on her, put her in a car and drive her away. Nothing matters any more. She and Miskis are finally and completely one. That is all.

~ ~ ~

The grizzly moves slowly up a steep slope that rises above Indian Creek. The sound of the gunfire reaches it clearly through the trees. The bear stops and turns in the direction of the firefight. The animal remains motionless for the long seconds of the barrage, the bear staring down towards the moving water and the killing only dimly visible many yards away. Sometime after the firing stops a light breeze carries the sharp bite of the gunsmoke to the grizzly's nose. On a ridge across from the bear a figure dressed in jeans, boots, wool shirt and coat moves silently and quickly away from the violence. The man's long, black, braided hair bounces on his back as he trots up hill. The grizzly sniffs in the man's direction catching his scent. Old genetic memories stir as the animal recognized his long-time foe and companion of the wide-open high plains where his kind used to roam centuries before. The figure disappears over the ridge. The grizzly tastes the air one more time and smells the dwindling scent of the warrior. The bear turns back on its course and works its way over the next ridge.

~ ~ ~

I haven't done much of anything for the last three weeks. Not since Miskis was killed. Nothing much at all after the cops drove down to Liz's house outside of Coltrane and arrested her, and charged her with Mark Grace's murder, along with Miskis. One gruesome detail surfaced during her lengthy interrogation and subsequent confession. She had helped dismember Grace with Sam's chainsaw. There'd been a good deal of conjecture among the cops and in the bars about how Grace had been cut up. Was it a Svea hand saw, a machete, a butcher knife or a chainsaw. The chainsaw edged out the knife in most arguments. Miskis did the killing. Afterwards she said she asked to take part in the ritual butchery. She'd used the Stihl right along with Miskis. Man, did I pick one crazy lady to fall for. For the time being, I decide to stick with trout, game birds and The Dog. I gave my story for the record to Qualls that same day. Then they all left me alone.

As I said, Liz gave her statement outlining the harsh

details of the whole thing. Signed off on it like she was no longer living among the rest of us, like an automaton, then was escorted to her cell. Nothing seemed to matter to her anymore. She avoided conversation with her court-appointed attorney, the guards, everyone. She just stared through them with a glassy-eyed expression of a zombie. Her last words to Qualls were "He and I are one now. There's nothing else." Nothing more. She'd turned silent like Sam, saying only one time to an officer bringing her breakfast that she loved Miskis and now they were together forever. A few days later Qualls came by and filled me in on the details of her confession. He saw that I was depressed enough already, told me to take care and that he'd call in a week or so and left. Dirt checks on me every day to see if I'm okay. He even comes by once in a while with a bottle of Jim Beam. He was a good friend and knows when to appear and when to stay away. Waukonda delivers groceries and beer each day and often a casserole. Each one smells so good - shrimp or morel mushrooms or smoked grouse in wild rice and cheese sauce or marinated elk - that I'm forced to abandon my self-pity inspired loss of appetite and gorge like a starved gourmand. The Count walks in each afternoon and takes The Dog down to the park next to the river where the two of them chase a bright green tennis ball for a couple of hours. They both are rounding into excellent shape. So, life moves on and I can see where I'll be returning to my normal routine within a week or so, Good friends in a nice small town are winning this small battle for me. I'm grateful.

What Liz and Miskis had done and the details of their life together upset me far more than being used by her.

Her scheme of diversion made sense and one thing she said to me lessened the sting. She said that even when she was forced to use a man for her needs, as she did the pool player years ago, she was only able to do so if she truly liked the guy. Small changes for a broken heart, but I've learned to take what's offered. I've been fine tuning that sad number all my adult life, but it's time to move on and quit the pathetic losing lover gig. We've all got our said songs to sing and I've grown damn sick of this one. No more.

Maybe they wanted to drive Sam nuts so she could gain control of his money through the power of attorney. We'll never know. Life often seems to be some elaborate chess game where the rules constantly change in throughout the play. Liz could have done the kind thing and simply murdered Sam. How could anyone think that it was better to drive him insane. Some of us are hopeless when it comes to women and we never seem to find the right one or when we do, we manage to destroy the relationship with the old standbys - booze, anger, insecurity and self-centeredness. I had this bunch down cold, and had lost the woman I really loved years ago. I planned on ridding myself of these traits. I hoped, even prayed, that I could, but I had my doubts, but, still, as Lyle Lovett once sang "You have to try."

I was surprised to see how quickly I recovered from my affair with Liz. Once I realized that there was only one woman I'd ever loved and it wasn't Liz, I came back to life in a hurry. Her madness and cold-heartedness overwhelmed any other feelings I'd had for her. The awful way they killed Grace and what they did to Sam is what got to me. Why do we do these things in our various ways and in our varying intensities? We're all sick at heart, I guess. Well, maybe not, but sometimes it seems that way.

Aside from what Liz told the police about the murder, and the wild game poaching and what they did to the Siksika bison herd, aside from this little bit of larceny, everything was pretty much over. When the cops poked through the charred remains of Miskis's cabin they didn't find much, a burned out freezer containing lots of trout and some buffalo steaks, piles of ruined books on hunting, and a wad of partially incinerated twenty-dollar bills. Liz told Qualls in the confession what little she knew about the tribal bison shootings, but that wasn't much. They did find an old refrigerator truck stored in the barn at Miskis's place and a bunch of camping and survival gear in his pickup. That was it. Nothing that could help the cops trace the meat to anyone else. He'd covered his tracks in every direction. It looked like Siksikas got a raw deal once again. Nothing about his life before Liz turned up, except that he'd been something of a roustabout over around Miles City for years. No record. No hint of trouble. The police over that way said he'd kept his nose clean. It did turn out that all of his records were falsified and as a result no one had a clue where he was from or what Miskis had done during his youth.

Charges were dropped against Sam and he'd been moved to the facility Moryn told Liz about, the one outside of Minneapolis. The doctor offered some hope that he'd recover, at least that's what he told me on the phone, but after what Sam had witnessed, I figured he was gone for good. Liz, or the shell of her body, would be going to prison. Miskis was dead. The remains now preserved in the state forensic lab in Helena for further study. The only open end was the arrow through Miskis's heart. The workmanship resembled that of the Northern Cheyenne, but their tribal officers failed to turn up anything on the Rez down by Lame Deer and Busby. Tribal authorities on the Siksika reservation made a perfunctory attempt at finding out something and called Qualls a few days after the shootout to report that they'd turned up a big fat zero. So that seemed to be the one remaining, and more than likely unsolved, part of the entire mess.

When I play all of the madness over in my head I always come to the conclusion that it had wound up as being pretty damn tidy for such an ugly situation. I'm angry and disappointed with myself for getting involved with Liz. I knew while all of this was happening that it wasn't right by the bad feeling I had in my stomach whenever I took an honest look at the situation, which wasn't often. Hell, plain old simple-minded common sense told me as much, but I was trying to put the loss of my Whitefish lady behind me and pretty much figured that whatever it took – booze, a dead-end relationship, whatever – was okay. Killing emotional time is a bad habit of mine. I wasn't willing to face the truth. At least I never got to the point where I even considered this to be a rational excuse, but more, perhaps at best, a slight explanation for pathetic behavior. Now it's time for me to move on to brighter moments in life. I reached this monumental decision a few days ago and have been feeling better and better. Still not ready to take on the world again, but I'm coming around and even working up to my old tricks with some new variations.

I walk over to the refrigerator and pull out a can of Guinness, then slide back to my desk. The Dog is sleeping in the closet. He's been keeping his distance lately, letting me work things out. Suddenly the door opens and in strolls the Count, still wearing his Octoberfest outfit. It's early for the two of them to go play ball at the park.

"My Indian friend just called and you'll never believe this. Talk about coincidence," I can see that The Count's on a roll. I can see it in his intensely sparkling eyes and on his flushed face. "The tribal police found Grover Loudermilk and someone named Bill Hands dead in Loudermilk's wrecked, burned-up truck. Seems they lost control, went off the road and plummeted close to a thousand feet down the Two Medicine gorge. Truck exploded burning the bodies some and what not. But isn't that queer, happening so soon after this terrible business around here?

"It's been no secret up there or with the state police, the FBI and the BIA that Loudermilk has been up to some shady dealings with the tribe, but no one's ever been able to pin anything down. The man's slippery as an eel."

I said that yes I'd heard all of that in pieces over the past few weeks and that I agreed with The Count. Maybe the tribal cops came up empty, but it appeared that other segments of the Siksikas had taken matters into their own hands and eliminated the bison herd manager. Reservations have their own laws and own way of doing things. What happens, happens, and outsiders never learn the real truth. That's the way that is, too. The Count could see that I still wasn't up to socializing, so he bowed, said goodbye and left. Lost control my ass, I thought. Members of the tribe, maybe members of their Contrary band, a wild bunch that did everything in life backwards from the rest of us, got even with Loudermilk and took an innocent bystander along with him. Well, the Siksika did have some catching up to do if they planned on evening the score with us. I felt bad for this Hands guy, but that's the way it goes sometimes.

Then Dirt shows up. He's was laughing like crazy. Apparently Biederbeck was up to speed today.

"Guess what happened over at the fly fishing museum?" he practically shouts. "When old man Zambrano opened the place up and turned on the lights, he almost had a stroke. Someone had removed all of the trout from the tanks and replaced them with carp. Isn't that great?"

I smile a little and say that I think that the move was a creative one. Perhaps a work of genius. At the very least, truly inspired.

Dirt looks at my smug grin, nods a bit and says "Okay."

"Enough of this feeling sorry for yourself nonsense. If your not at my place for Happy Hour tonight by six, we're all coming down here to get you. For real."

I say "Okay I'll come up for a few, but that's all."

After Dirt leaves, I laugh out loud about the trout and the carp. I wonder who could have done such a thing. I'm, feeling much better and flicked on the CD player – Amos Garrett's Cold Creek Club. Great music. Even The Dog wanders out. He gives me a quick once over and decides that I'm showing definite signs of coming back to life. He jumps up on the couch with a grunt, turns in circles for awhile, crumples in a heap and falls asleep.

The phone rings.

"Hello."

"Ed? How are you doing?" It's the voice of the woman I thought I'd never hear from again. My Whitefish lady. A jolt of pure electrical joy rips through me from brain to toes. The woman has radar that is beyond description and quite possible unique among our species, at least to my mind's eye. And as is probably appropriate, I can't think of a word to say to her after all these years. "Are you okay? I've been worried about you. One of those feelings I get, you know."

I'm still at a loss for words and there is the wildly happy sound of her laughter ringing in my ear.

"Don't hurt yourself there, Ed." She said. "I'm coming down day after tomorrow, as soon as I get some new tires put on the Scout.

"You know buddy, despite all of that insane time spent fly fishing and your commitment to writing at times at all costs, and even the drinking, I've realized that I've missed you a lot. Yeah, a lot. So much for my good judgment, but I really do love you and want to see you again. So, tell me, how the hell are you doing?"

"As of right now, just fine," I say.

-30-

Thank you for reading.
Please review this book. Reviews help others find New
Pulp Press and inspire us to keep providing these
marvelous tales.

If you would like to be put on our email list to receive
updates on new releases, contests, and promotions, please
go to NewPulpPress.com and sign up.

About the Author

John Holt spends as much time as possible fishing and hanging out in sparsely-populated country with his wife, photographer Ginny Holt, mainly the remoteness found on northern high plains east of the continental divide in Montana and connected country that runs north into the Yukon and Northwest Territories. They've done numerous articles for a variety of magazines including *The Flyfish Journal, Crossroads, Men's Journal, Big Sky Journal, American Cowboy* and *The Art of Angling Journal* on their experiences on the road. Acquiring vintage reels and bamboo fly rods and smoking top shelf cigars are other interests.. He and Ginny recently completed the book *Fly Fishing Montana.* Other titles the two have done include *Coyote Nowhere – In Search of America's Last Frontier, Yellowstone Drift – Floating the Past in Real Time, Arctic Aurora – Canada's Yukon and Northwest Territories* and *Stalking Trophy Browns.* They live in Livingston, Montana.

http://www.newpulppress.com/

www.ingramcontent.com/pod-product-compliance
Lightning Source LLC
Chambersburg PA
CBHW070447260626
47161CB00004B/1230